SEC

"Hello, you've reached the K-LAU request line," Kim said as she picked up the station phone.

"Is this Kim?" a boy asked.

"Yes, who's this?"

"A friend."

The boy was deliberately trying to disguise his voice. He sounded nice, though, and sort of attractive. "OK, friend," she said. "What can I do for you?"

"I'd like you to play my favorite song, 'Every Breath You Take' by the Police."

"And would you like to dedicate it to someone?"

"Yes. To you, Kim."

"Why, thank you, um—who did you say you were?"

All Kim heard was a click and the dial tone.

Secret Admirer

Debra Spector

BANTAM BOOKS

TORONTO • NEW YORK • LONDON • SYDNEY • AUCKLAND

RL 6, IL age 11 and up

SECRET ADMIRER
A Bantam Book / April 1985

ISBN 0-553-24688-7

Published simultaneously in the United States and Canada

---

*Bantam Books are published by Bantam Books, Inc. Its trademark,
consisting of the words "Bantam Books" and the portrayal of a
rooster, is registered in U.S. Patent and Trademark Office and in
other countries. Marca Registrada. Bantam Books, Inc., 666 Fifth
Avenue, New York, New York 10103.*

Printed and bound in Great Britain by Hunt Barnard Printing Ltd.

O 0 9 8 7 6 5 4 3 2 1

Secret Admirer

Chapter One

"Good afternoon, everyone. This is Kim Belding rocking with you on a gorgeous Monday. All of you out there better be good, 'cause I'm coming at you with the law—K-LAU, that is, the best and brashest radio station in the country. I'll be with you for the next hour, playing all your favorites and keeping you up to date on all the latest happenings here at Laurence High School. Just keep your ears open and your feet ready to dance, 'cause we're going to start out today with an old one from David Bowie."

Kim signaled through the glass partition to Rodney Hartung, the engineer sitting at the control booth in the next room, to start the record. Then she sat back on the frayed red vinyl swivel chair and sighed. "Whew, I didn't think I was going to get up here in time," she said into the intercom as soon as Rodney cut off her mike. "Mrs. Schroeder kept us after class to go over

1

French verbs. *Quel dommage!* I had to run to make it."

Rodney looked through the large plate-glass window and shook his head. "Maybe you ought to switch to a closer French class."

"Or give it up completely. I'm spending half the class thinking about the show, anyway."

She could have said that for any of her other classes as well. Not that she was in danger of failing anything, but Kim didn't find the same excitement in discussing frogs or analyzing T.S. Eliot as she did in planning a radio program down to the last second. That was a real challenge. Anyone could memorize the stuff needed to get through classes, but creating an interesting program from scratch took real skill.

At sixteen Kim felt she had that skill—or at least was well on her way to developing it. Kim lived and breathed radio, having made up her mind at age five that she was going to be a disc jockey when she grew up. Nothing that had happened since had changed her mind. The year before, she was one of only two tenth graders to get on the station staff. She'd decided she had a good chance of being on the air if she could do something original. Since she didn't have a crazy enough personality to do radio comedy, Kim culled through her vast collection of records and put together an audition tape filled with little-known songs by various rock groups. Her

"Something Different" show had turned out to be very popular with Laurence students.

This year she had worked herself up to a three-day shift. She was on the air every Monday, Wednesday, and Friday. She wished she could be on every day, but Mr. Block, the station faculty adviser, wanted to give as many students as possible a chance to get on-the-air experience, and he wouldn't allow anyone on more than three times a week.

Still, Kim felt she had no right to complain. Actually she felt downright fortunate that her parents had settled in Laurence. The small southern California town was one of only about eighteen in the state that supported a high-school-run radio station. During the mornings the studio and the auxiliary production studio were used for classes and workshop practice. KLAU itself operated twelve hours a day, from noon to midnight. Included in its programming were a high-school equivalency program that ran from eight to midnight and a classical music show that was on from noon to two-thirty. The rest of the time the station belonged to the students, and, except for a newscast that ran from five to five-thirty, they filled the airwaves with rock music.

Kim was pleased with the program she'd planned that day. Kim liked to vary her shows, mixing some Top Forty songs in with the lesser known rock numbers. Most of the time she spent her study periods planning her shows, pulling records from the high-school station's record library and putting them in the box reserved for her in the adjacent student office.

While the Bowie song was still playing, Kim signaled Rodney to cue up the next record from the stack she'd piled on the Formica counter behind him. With lightning speed he had it on the turntable and ready to play. "The Clash," he said, reading the label. "Going for the fast stuff, huh?"

"You bet. I feel like dancing today," she said, bouncing around on her seat.

While Kim was repositioning her headphones, Rodney took a prerecorded cartridge from the rack in front of him and slipped it into the tape machine. A voice saying, "Let's party," went out over the air.

Kim smiled and flashed an OK sign to Rodney. The engineer wasn't handsome and didn't attract much attention around school, but Kim had come to like him in the several months he'd been working as her engineer.

Rodney did all the behind-the-scenes work that enabled Kim to run her show smoothly, things like opening and closing her microphone, cueing up the records and tapes, watching the VU meter and "riding gain" so the levels of music and voice were neither too high nor too low. He was a whiz at the controls, too. Unlike some student engineers who never could cue up records properly, Rodney was a master at the equipment. And, as if that weren't enough, he always seemed to come up with clever sound effects. Kim was impressed by his skill. "Say, when is the Rodney Hartung show going to make its debut?" she asked, as she had several times before.

As always, whenever she asked this question, Rodney turned red. Not just his face, but his hands and neck, too. "Never," he said in a whisper.

Kim couldn't understand why a guy like Rodney would be so afraid of stepping before the microphone. One of the things she loved best about radio was its anonymity. "It's the theater of the mind," Mr. Block was fond of saying. Radio allowed the audience to use its imagination, to form ideas about the disc jockey based on voice alone. No listener had to know what the deejay looked like, and that was something Kim truly appreciated.

Not that she felt she had anything to hide. Though not beautiful in a sensational way, Kim was attractive. She wore her short-cropped brown hair swept back, which allowed her brown eyes to dominate her fair-skinned face. Her small, kittenish nose was perfectly suited to her thin face and slender, petite body.

Kim preferred to go by her own name on the air, but some students at Laurence chose to take on other identities. There was one disc jockey named Sean Englund, who did a show every Saturday evening as Rex Corona, the mad teenager. Rex had a storehouse of crazy, weird voices, and he mixed up his music sets with hysterically funny interviews. In real life, though, Sean was so quiet that Kim didn't realize he was in her English class until Ms. Frankel called on him two weeks into the semester. He didn't ever like to be seen speaking to Kim in class, on the off chance that someone might make the connection and figure out he was involved in KLAU. Sean wanted to keep his radio identity a secret from the rest of the school, and he had succeeded wonderfully.

Now, running her fingers through her hair, Kim told Rodney, "I don't know what you're scared of. The station's signal can only be heard in Laurence. It's not like you're broadcasting to the entire country."

"But don't you ever get nervous thinking about all those people out there listening?"

"Of course I get a little nervous just before the show starts, but I don't let it bother me. I don't think about all those people listening when I talk into the mike. I just pretend I'm talking to myself."

"I know I couldn't do that. Say, Kim, when you turn pro, could you take me along as your engineer?"

"We'll see, Rodney," she said because she knew she couldn't make any promises. She'd learned that lots of stations made their disc jockeys engineer their own shows. Even a lot of the big-name jocks in nearby San Diego did their shows solo. Kim was learning how to operate the control board in her radio production class, but she hardly got enough time to master it during class, and recently she'd begun skipping lunches to get in more practice time.

Her good friend and usual lunch partner, Jennifer Biondi, couldn't understand that kind of devotion, and even Kim's parents had a hard time dealing with her obsession for radio. They had never been too pleased with her being a disc jockey and hoped it was just a phase she'd grow out of. But when she began to talk about skipping college and trying to get a job right out of high school, they were horrified. The matter had been settled only when Kim decided to go to college and major in broadcasting.

But radio wasn't only serious business for Kim; it was a lot of fun, too. After her show was over, she would often hang out with some of the other volunteers who worked at the station. She'd talk about music or help sort out the record library. Other times she helped her friend Lisa Vonder, who was the news director, put together the newscast. Kim loved the spirit of camaraderie that existed among the station staff. Everyone was working hard to make KLAU sound as good as it could.

Just then Kim spotted Vic Pastore, the student station manager, darting into the control room with a stack of cartridges. More than anyone else, Vic was responsible for KLAU's relaxed and somewhat irreverent format. Kim knew this better than anyone. She had spent many long nights working beside him when the two of them had been dating. That was the year before, soon after Kim had joined the station staff.

Looking at Vic, Kim could hardly believe how much she'd thought she was in love with him then. She realized now that it hadn't been love at all, just infatuation with the first guy who'd appreciated her talent. Vic had been a sort of tutor to Kim, and often their dates were spent right there at the radio station, talking about music and formats and different ways to "talk up" a record. It was fun at first, but gradually Kim realized she wanted more from a boyfriend than shop talk.

Kim finally broke up with Vic at the beginning of the school year. When she told him the news, Vic had just shrugged and said that it was no big deal. That had gotten Kim so angry that she'd hardly spoken to him since, except for station matters.

Nevertheless, Kim was still proud of the way Vic ran the station. But not everyone at Laurence shared her feelings. For months, Heather Shearson, the editor of the Laurence *Messenger*, the school newspaper, had been running editorials critical of KLAU and had been leading a campaign to remove Vic as station manager. Kim resented Heather's interference. After Heather's first attack in the *Messenger* the year before, when Kim and Vic were still dating, Kim had tried to raise Vic's spirits with a T-shirt she had had made up that said "I am a Renegade from the LAU." Vic had liked the shirt so much that he had given one to her, too.

Kim was wearing her shirt that day. She still considered it one of her most prized possessions. She liked the idea of being thought of as a renegade, although she had never done anything to earn an outlaw image. Except for her self-admitted outlandish wardrobe, which included everything from suede miniskirts to baggy men's suits, she was as conventional as most girls in her class.

A rap on the window from Rodney interrupted Kim's thoughts, and she sat up and signaled him to open her mike. "That was Prince on the LAU. And this is Kim Belding with you until three-thirty. Our request line is now open. If you want to hear any of your favorites, call us at five-five-five-zero-zero-three-four. That's five-five-five-zero-zero-three-four. Now here's something old but good from Mr. Lou Reed."

Kim got quite a few requests for songs. Her biggest audience was over at the Clubhouse, a coffee shop across the street that was a popular after-school gathering place. They always had the station on, and the kids tied up the pay phone there with requests. But Kim tried to limit the requests to three per show; if she responded to all the requests she received, she would never get to play the music she'd planned so carefully.

As soon as the song faded out, Kim began to talk again. As she spoke, Rodney started a tape in the background playing the old Ramones' song, "Rock and Roll High School."

"Kim Belding back with you for one of the more popular segments of our show—Schoolbeat, where we keep you up to date on all the latest school happenings. Here's what's going on this week." Kim glanced at the papers in front of her. "Friday night at eight, the Laurence Lancers go against those big bad bruisers from Wilson High. The Lancers are undefeated so far this season, but Wilson is always tough. So get out and cheer for your favorite players. That's eight o'clock Friday night at the stadium." Deviating from her prepared script, Kim added, "Now personally I think football is too violent, but if you're into seeing guys get knocked around for fun, go out and cheer them on."

Returning to a more serious voice, Kim continued. "Do you like to sing? The Glee Club is having tryouts next Monday after school in the auditorium. The Chess Club meets tomorrow after school in Room one-seventeen, and the French Club is having a meeting Wednesday in Room two-eighteen. Also on Wednesday there's a

meeting of the junior prom fund-raising committee. That's in the band room.

"And last but not least, don't forget there's an
assembly tomorrow morning. Principal O'Malley
will be handing out this year's Laurence Community Achievement Award. One of Laurence's
top students will be honored for the contributions he or she's made in making Laurence a
better place to live." Improvising again, Kim
added caustically, "I understand this year's special honor will be bestowed on our illustrious
student council president, Mr. Buddy Forward.
We're proud of you, Buddy, real proud," she said,
letting the sarcasm rise in her voice. "And, listeners, because he's been such a good friend of
K-LAU, I want to take this opportunity to extend
my congratulations. What do you say, gang?
Join with me in giving Buddy a hand." Kim
pointed a finger at Rodney, who punched up a
cartridge of a chorus of boos.

Kim was still chuckling as she introduced the
next song. Obviously, Buddy Forward was no
friend of hers or the station's. Kim had hoped
that, as the leading student in school, Buddy
would defend KLAU against Heather Shearson's
attacks. But he hadn't said one word in defense
of the station. In a way, Kim shouldn't have been
surprised about that. Buddy seemed to have
blinders on when it came to Heather. They used
to date each other the year before. And even
though he'd broken up with her, Buddy still

acted as if Heather could do no wrong. If she had a complaint about the station, then it was clear to him which party was at fault. Kim felt her little "editorial" was the least she could do in return.

A phone call broke into her thoughts. "Hello, you've reached the K-LAU request line," she answered. "May I help you?"

"Is this Kim?" a boy asked.

"Yes, who's this?"

"A friend."

Kim had no idea who it was. The boy was deliberately trying to disguise his voice. He sounded nice, though, and sort of attractive. "OK, friend," she said. "What can I do for you?"

"I'd like you to play my favorite song, 'Every Breath You Take' by the Police."

"And would you like to dedicate it to someone?"

"Yes. To you, Kim."

She was surprised to hear that. "Why, thank you, um—who did you say you were?"

All she heard was a click and the dial tone.

Chapter Two

Kim was still thinking about her mysterious phone call the following morning when she, Lisa, and Jennifer took their seats for the general assembly. She'd never before had anyone dedicate a song to her, especially a love song.

Kim glanced slowly around the packed auditorium. Somewhere in that very room, there was someone who probably had his eyes focused on her, and it was driving her crazy not to know who it was.

The only one who seemed curious about what she was doing was Jennifer. "Who are you looking for?" she asked.

"My secret admirer," Kim told her.

Jennifer nudged her with her elbow. "Come on, stop teasing me. We both know that secret admirers don't exist."

"Well, maybe you're wrong." Kim told her

13

about the phone call. "And I've got to find out who it is."

Lisa gave Kim a sharp jab in the side as she looked up at the stage. "Shh! Our fearless leader is about to speak."

Kim turned her eyes to the stage, where Principal O'Malley was beginning her speech on the virtues of public service. Sitting on a metal folding chair to her right was Buddy Forward.

"I've heard this speech a million times. You're taping it, aren't you?" Kim asked.

Lisa nodded, her straight brown bangs flopping into her eyes. "Yes, my machine's right under the podium. But I'm really more interested in Buddy's speech. I'll probably use a couple of cuts on tonight's news." She shrugged her slim shoulders apologetically. "It's a slow day."

"Do you really expect Mr. Goody-Two-Shoes to say anything interesting?" Jennifer asked.

Kim answered for Lisa. "Miracles *can* happen, Jennifer."

Jennifer giggled. "From Buddy? Laurence's own Boy Wonder? What do you think he's going to lecture about this time?"

"I have no idea. But first we'll have to suffer through the Big O," Lisa said, then groaned.

Principal O'Malley's loud voice boomed over the overamplified microphone. "Our young people are our most precious resource, and we at Laurence High School are proud to honor a very special young man . . ."

"Forget Buddy," Kim hissed, keeping her voice low so she couldn't be heard by her homeroom teacher at the far end of the row. "I'm serious about that phone call. I wonder who's interested in me?"

"Seems to me if he were really interested he'd have told you his name."

". . . a familiar face to everyone," Ms. O'Malley continued. "A hard worker both in school and in the community, a boy who has given of himself in many charity drives . . ."

"Not necessarily," Kim said, ignoring the principal's speech. "It's obvious to me that the guy's really shy. Why else would he go to all the trouble of disguising his voice? He's probably afraid of rejection or something. But if I can figure out who he is, maybe I could give him a sign I'm interested."

"But how do you know if you are?" Jennifer asked. "I mean, what if he turned out to be someone like Buddy Forward?"

". . . who has worked tirelessly on behalf of the Laurence Community Chest, who volunteered to clean up after last spring's flash floods . . ."

"I could always say no," Kim said. "But even if Dracula asked me out, I might say yes. I haven't had a date since Vic and I split up. And I'm ready."

"Without further ado, let me present this year's Laurence Community Achiever, Buddy Forward."

15

The applause that erupted throughout the auditorium jolted the three girls into facing the stage. They watched with passing interest as Buddy took his place behind the podium, a warm smile on his face. There was no doubt that a lot of people at Laurence High looked up to the attractive, blond-haired senior, whose clean-cut looks were enhanced by the dark blue suit he wore.

While he waited for the applause to die down, Kim looked around the room again. This time her gaze met Heather Shearson's. The red-haired girl glared back at her with cold green eyes, silently scolding Kim for not clapping. Even though they were no longer the golden couple of Laurence High, Heather still felt protective of Buddy.

"Heather's giving me the old evil eye," Kim quipped to Jennifer as Buddy began his acceptance speech.

"If you don't keep quiet and listen to his speech, you're going to be on her enemy list forever," Lisa cut in.

"I can see it now. A banner headline in next week's *Messenger:* 'Kim Belding Snubs Buddy Forward.' I'm sure Heather's looking for an excuse to roast me—or anyone at K-LAU for that matter."

"I thought she'd cooled off on her 'get K-LAU' campaign," Jennifer said.

"Just because she's done one issue without

roasting us? Huh-uh. That's what she wants you to believe," Kim replied. "The way I see it, it's not enough for her to be in charge of the *Messenger* and coeditor of the yearbook. She won't be satisfied until she and her friend control everything in this school."

Buddy began to speak. "I can't accept this award without thanking everyone who has worked with me. I could never have accomplished anything without the help of my friends."

"Friends like his I wouldn't wish on anyone," Kim continued. "I mean, can you imagine what would happen if Heather got control of K-LAU? She'd turn it into the same empty nonsense the *Messenger* has become."

"Yeah," piped up Jennifer. "Nothing but Barry Manilow and lots of Linda Ronstadt's slow stuff."

"Hey, will you guys keep quiet?" A boy sitting behind Kim hissed in her ear. "Some of us are interested in what Buddy has to say."

"Sorry," Kim whispered back.

"Maybe if you listened, you'd learn something," the boy continued.

"I doubt it," Kim retorted.

Kim hated it when other people tried to tell her what was good for her. She'd be the one to determine whether Buddy had anything relevant to say to her. Knowing his track record, she thought listening would be a waste of time. She was sure Buddy's only goal in life was to accumulate as many extracurricular activities credits as possible in order to impress a college admissions official. She figured Buddy must have reached his quota by now. Besides the student council, he was an active contributor to the *Messenger* and was on the prom committee, president of the Science Club, and played on the school soccer team. This award he was getting was just another feather in an already crowded cap.

Kim didn't care to hear him brag about his accomplishments. It didn't help matters any that she was missing radio production, her favorite class, to be here. But try as she could to tune out Buddy's speech, what he was saying caught Kim's attention.

"I believe Laurence would be a much better school if all of its students involved themselves in worthwhile activities. What you perhaps don't realize is how much you stand to gain by participating."

That much I can agree with, Kim thought. She got great satisfaction from participating in the radio station activities.

"Of course we have to distinguish between worthwhile contributions and those that do nothing but satisfy egos. This is especially true if you involve yourself in an activity that puts you in the spotlight. I'm not here to criticize, but there are some students at Laurence who seem to enjoy using school facilities and the public airwaves as their own personal forums. They're not here to inform or to educate, but to show off their talents—and I might add, not too well—and to show us all how important they are. They are taking a vital public airway and using it for selfish purposes. . . ."

Now, wait a minute, Buddy, Kim raged inwardly. She had no idea why now, of all times, he had decided to join Heather's war against the radio station. She knew she was performing a valuable service, and she thought the rest of the station staff was doing the same. Sure, everyone had personal tastes, but that's what made the station lively. Besides, the station was open to anyone else through the request lines. Even Buddy had been offered the opportunity to broadcast news from the student council. But he had declined for some reason. And now he was attacking the station for being unfair.

Kim hunched forward and listened with rapt attention to Buddy's words. Nothing could get her to talk to her friends now. A few moments later it became clear what was behind Buddy's attack.

"It is one thing to foist narrow musical tastes onto a mass audience, which is unacceptable but at least understandable. But what cannot be tolerated are events such as one that happened yesterday, when a certain air personality on K-LAU took it in her hands to launch a verbal attack against me, a series of potshots that humiliated me in front of the entire town. I was not even given a chance to defend myself. . . ."

What's he talking about? Kim wondered. It was clear Buddy was referring to the joking remark she'd made during her program. But to call it a humiliating attack? He must have skin as thin as cellophane to come to such a far-fetched conclusion as that.

She felt a tug on her sleeve from Jennifer. "He's attacking you," her friend declared. "Aren't you going to do something about it?"

Kim's mind was racing frantically. But she cautioned herself to stay calm and not to over-react. "Now isn't the time, Jennifer," Kim said. "If this is Buddy's declaration of war, I'm ready to defend myself. But on my terms, not his. I'll find a way."

The following afternoon, during her program, Kim got her revenge. As she closed her show, she began her own congratulatory speech to Buddy. "I can't leave today without commenting on yesterday's award assembly. We here at K-LAU believe in free expression and invite anyone who wants to contribute to our programming. Our request lines have been open since the beginning of the show, and you've heard several of the songs called in by our listeners. Now I'm going to deviate a little and close the show with a dedication of my own. This next song is dedicated to yesterday's hero, our own student council president, Buddy Forward. And a most appropriate one at that. Here's to you, Bud."

Increasing in volume behind her was Adam Ant singing "Goody Two Shoes."

Chapter Three

Kim gazed at the clock on the wall of her American history class and silently counted the remaining seconds in the period. History class always seemed to drag on forever, but that day it felt as if Mr. Ballard would continue his lecture into the next century. But that was because Kim was more anxious than usual for class to end. The station had received the new Wild Rider album that morning, and she planned to listen to it during her lunch period immediately following class.

Three—two—one. At exactly eleven forty-five Kim bolted from her seat and headed for the door. She was already out in the hall, about to make a mad dash for the stairs, when she heard a voice behind her. A *male* voice. "Hey, Kim, got a second?"

Kim stopped in her tracks and turned around. Ray Rollins, a tall, slim boy with dark, wavy hair that he wore slicked back off his face, walked hesitantly toward her. Kim hardly knew him; he was a recent transfer student who sat quietly in the back row. She wondered what he wanted. "If it's about the homework, forget it," she said, staring into his blue eyes. "I slept through class."

"No, it's nothing like that," he said, starting to grin. "I have a favor to ask you."

Responding to Kim's open expression, Ray moved closer. All Kim could see in front of her was the picture on his Stray Cats T-shirt. She edged backward a little until she found herself leaning against a water fountain. "I'll try to help if I can."

Ray moved forward a step. "I'm new here at school, so you may not know that I front a band called Rockin' Rollins. The guys and I are going to be playing Friday night at Grandma's Palace, and I'd like you to put in a plug for us on your next show."

Kim had never gotten a request like that before, but she had no objections to helping out a new band. "Be glad to." She smiled. "What kind of music do you play?"

"A little of everything, from hard rock to slow stuff. My show stopper is 'Every Breath You Take.' It's my favorite song. People tell me I sound just like Sting, too."

"Really?"

"Course I don't look like him, but what's a fellow to do." Ray smiled a little sheepishly as the bell rang. "I guess I'm keeping you from class."

Kim shook her head. "Don't worry. It's my lunch period, but I was headed up to the station to listen to the new Wild Rider album."

"I didn't know they had one."

"Hot off the presses. It's not in the stores yet. Would you like to hear it with me?" Kim hadn't planned on company, but the invitation just slipped out naturally. Ray seemed like someone worth getting to know better.

The tall boy looked disappointed. "Wish I could, but I've got a test next period. Anyway, I hope you can come see us Friday."

"I'll try," Kim said as she walked away. It wasn't until she'd reached the third floor that it dawned on her that "Every Breath You Take" was her mystery caller's favorite song, too.

When she arrived at the station entrance, she found Buddy Forward waiting by the door. As soon as he spotted her, he scowled angrily.

Buddy was the last person she wanted to see. Trying to ignore him, Kim reached for the doorknob. Buddy put his hand over hers.

"You couldn't leave well enough alone, could you?" His normally friendly voice was hard.

"I don't know what you're talking about, Buddy," Kim answered, her voice as cool as a Popsicle. "Now will you let me through?"

"Not yet," he said, still holding the doorknob. "I want to talk to you, Kim."

"I'm busy," she replied. "Maybe later." *Like around 1999*, she added to herself.

"You seem to have plenty of time to knock me on the air. What's the matter, don't you have the guts to do it to my face?"

"I suppose I could say the same about you, couldn't I?" she challenged. "That was quite a speech you gave the other day." She took her hand off the knob. "Look, I've got things to do, so whatever you have to say, say it quickly."

"OK," Buddy said. "I think you owe me an apology—and I want it now."

"For what?" Kim demanded.

"When someone gets their name slurred before an entire town, I think they deserve the chance to have their name cleared. Don't you?" Buddy's blue eyes bore down on Kim.

She refused to be intimidated. "If you're talking about yesterday's show—and I assume you are—then I'd say you're one remarkably thin-skinned person. All I did was dedicate a song to you, and I'd hardly call that a slur. As a matter of fact, I thought I went pretty lightly on you, considering the way you embarrassed me at the assembly."

"*I* embarrassed *you*? I did you a favor, Kim, by not mentioning your name. Unfortunately, I can't say the same thing about you."

"I'm not the one who stood up in front of the

entire school and accused a certain disc jockey of slander. You think I considered that a compliment?" she cried.

"You think I enjoyed being the punch lines of your feeble jokes?" Buddy's voice was rising in anger.

"What jokes?" Kim yelled. Then, realizing she could be heard all over the third floor, she lowered her voice. "All I did was have a little fun with your getting that award—as if all you needed from this school was another trophy."

"What's that supposed to mean? What's wrong with someone getting recognized for doing something useful around here? I happen to be proud of that award, and I resent it when you knock it on our own school station. It's not fair."

"What are you getting so steamed up about? I didn't do anything to damage your *illustrious* reputation. Like I said, I was just having fun, and I never thought you'd take that stuff so seriously. After all, a public figure like you has to expect some criticism once in a while—and be man enough to handle it."

"Humph," he snorted. "Heather told me you'd try to get out of this."

"Heather," Kim said angrily. "It figures she's behind this."

"She had nothing to do with it. It was my idea to see you."

"Well, for the record, Buddy, I'm not trying to get out of anything. I'm only trying to defend myself—and that goes for your attack on the rest of the station staff, too. I don't really care what you think about my show and me, but I don't think it's fair for you to put down the rest of the station. For your information, a lot of people around here like what we do, no matter what your friend Heather tells you. As far as I'm concerned, if you don't like what you hear, don't listen. No one's making you."

"I never listen, anyway. I'm too busy."

"Then how did you know what I said about you?"

"Heather told me."

Heather was at it again, trying to stir up more trouble for KLAU. Kim felt she had to stop it now. An idea suddenly occurred to her. "Hmmm, we definitely need to talk about this. Let's go inside and sit down." Kim opened the door to the station complex. Buddy took it from her and held it open, motioning with his free arm for her to enter first. Kim looked at him oddly as she walked inside the small, cluttered room that served as the station's front office and reception area.

Buddy followed quickly, and before Kim had a chance to act, he pulled a folding chair from the wall and opened it up for her against the desk space at the back of the room. "Why, you're a regular Sir Galahad, aren't you!" she noted with a curious mixture of sarcasm and surprised appreciation. "I thought that kind of chivalry went out centuries ago," Kim added, surprised to find something likable about Buddy. At least she no longer felt like ignoring him.

Buddy shrugged. "What can I say? I was born polite." He smiled as he took a seat for himself, setting it against the wall opposite Kim.

"Then what's a nice, polite guy like you doing going around and accusing me of slandering you?"

"Well, Heather said—"

"What exactly did she tell you? Did you ever think she might be wrong?"

"I doubt that *Heather*—"

Kim cut him off as her anger began to rise once again. "Oh, yes, Heather Shearson, president of the Laurence Honor Society, editor of the newspaper, big brain of the senior class. She could *never* be wrong. Her word against mine, a lowly junior, who has to struggle to get good grades. Obviously a loser in your eyes. Not to mention a member of the unmentionably horrible K-LAU. Why it's no contest. But just for the record, could you repeat what Heather told you I said?"

Buddy shifted uncomfortably in his chair. "I can't quote her exactly. But she told me you questioned my ability to lead the student council. She said you made a fool out of me."

Kim started to laugh. "What's so funny?" Buddy wanted to know.

She didn't answer right away. Instead, getting

up from her chair, she jogged down the narrow hallway into the production studio and fingered through a metal rack until she found what she wanted. Then she took the reel of tape and set it up on the reel-to-reel machine to the side of the control panel.

By this time Buddy had ventured down the hallway after her. Peering through the open door to the control room he asked, "What are you doing?"

"Defending myself," Kim said. Returning her attention to the machine in front of her, she pressed the fast-forward button and watched the tape wind around the take-up reel. "This is an air check of my show," she said. She flicked a few switches on the control board before pressing the play button on the machine. The sound of her amplified voice filled the room.

Buddy was shocked. "You're not playing this on the air again, are you?"

"I'm not stupid, Buddy." She pointed to the board, mildly exasperated. "This is the production room. The main studio is down at the end of the hall." The tape was approaching the remarks she'd made about Buddy. "Now listen." The two of them stood silently as the tape replayed her words. After her lead in to the song "Goody Two Shoes," Kim stopped the tape. "Now, Judge Forward, I ask you. Are those grounds for slander?"

"Strictly speaking, no, I suppose they're not. But they *are* unfair."

"No more so than your remarks about me—and the station." Kim started to rewind the tape and switched off the board.

Buddy watched the effortless movement of her fingers. "You really know how to run this stuff?"

Kim's exasperation level moved up a notch. "We radio people aren't dummies, Judge Forward."

"Would you please stop calling me judge?"

"Only when you stop labeling me and my friends undesirables. Just how much do you know about the radio station, anyway? Or the people who run it?"

"I know enough to know you don't represent the interests of everyone at school. You're a closed group interested only in playing music you like with no consideration for anyone else's tastes. If you ask me, I think it's a waste of a valuable resource."

"I could say the same thing about the *Messenger*," Kim retorted. "But I won't because I'm not going to dignify your attack with a reply."

"That's because you know I'm right," Buddy said.

"You happen to be one hundred percent wrong," Kim answered. "Anyone who thinks our shows are all alike obviously hasn't listened to us very closely. This station is probably more representative of the Laurence student body than any other organization around here. It's made up of lots of individuals who have their own ideas about how things should be. I hardly ever see most of these people outside of the station. But that doesn't matter because something special happens when we all walk through those doors. When we're here together, we're like a family. We're all committed to the same thing, trying to make this station work. Vic has worked like crazy to make us sound as professional as possible. He's the best station manager this school has ever had. He's put his mark on the station, much in the same way that Heather has put her own mark on the newspaper. Or even you on the student council.

"I'll tell you this much, Buddy," Kim continued, "I love working here, and I'm not ashamed to admit I probably spend more time at the station than I do for any of my classes. Every time I walk in here I feel a sense of magic. This is the place where I can shine. I'm sorry if you feel what I do is unimportant. If you don't like it, you don't have to listen to it. But don't ever tell me that I have no right to be here."

"I'm not trying to get you off the air, Kim," Buddy said. "But I'd like to hear other viewpoints on the air, too."

"Frankly, so would I. But contrary to what you might think, we don't have people lining up outside waiting to go on the air. Most kids here would much rather listen to the station than be on it. Even your friend Heather is welcome to audition a show if she wants. But she

31

seems interested only in attacking, not in participating."

"I doubt you'd let her have a program," Buddy said.

"I don't make those decisions around here. But it seems to me you were offered a chance to go on and talk about the student council. How come you haven't done so?"

"I—I have my reasons," Buddy stammered, his voice lacking some of his earlier forcefulness.

"Like what?" Kim demanded.

"Like I don't want to tell you," Buddy said.

Kim shrugged. "OK, I think I'm a fair person, Buddy. If you feel I've done you a disservice, I'll let you come on my show and speak. How does tomorrow sound? You'll be able to defend yourself all you want."

"What about the apology?"

Kim stood firm. "I have nothing to apologize for," she said, shaking her head. "So, will you be here?"

Buddy looked uncomfortable. "I'd rather hear you say you're sorry about what you said."

Kim snorted. "What's the matter, Buddy? Too busy to stick up for yourself? If you can't find the time, I guess it must not be very important to you after all."

"That's not true!" Buddy said.

"Then be here at the studio tomorrow at three-fifteen sharp. Now if you'll excuse me, I've got some things to do before the period's over." She turned her back on Buddy, indicating that as far as she was concerned, the conversation was over.

"OK," she heard him say after a long pause.

Kim shook her head as Buddy walked away. She thought he'd have jumped at the chance to go on the air. His reluctance to defend himself surprised her. *Strange,* she concluded. *Very strange indeed.*

Chapter Four

The call came five minutes into Kim's show. "Hi, Kim," the boy whispered. "Is the request line open yet?"

"Not officially," she answered, "but I'll take your request. What would you like to hear?"

The boy was still whispering. His voice sounded a little hoarse, too, as if he had laryngitis—or he was trying to disguise it. "How about something from the new Wild Rider album?"

Kim's heart began to pound. Ever since their encounter in the hallway, she'd begun to suspect that her mystery caller was Ray Rollins. The notion was hardly an unpleasant one. She'd felt comfortable with Ray's easygoing manner. She wouldn't mind getting to know him better; in fact, the more she'd thought about it, the more she felt he might be the guy she'd been waiting for all this time.

The call only confirmed her suspicions. There weren't many people who knew about the album—or that she had it. But Ray did. "Who is this?" she asked, trying to sound as offhand as possible. "Do I know you?"

The boy chuckled softly. "I think so," he said. "You have nineteen questions left."

"So you like to play games. OK. Does that mean that after I ask you another nineteen questions, you'll tell me who you are?"

"Maybe. Eighteen left."

"What does that mean?" she asked.

"You'll have to figure that out. Seventeen."

Kim glanced quickly at the clock. She didn't have time to rattle off that many questions. Trying to sound as cool as possible, she said, "Look, I've got to have your name. As in 'so-and-so requests this song.' Do you want to play it for anyone special? I like to say that, too, when I lead into the songs."

"Oh, I know that, Kim. I listen to you all the time. Just say that a friend is requesting it for you."

Kim almost strained her ear trying to identify the voice. Whoever it was was doing a great disguising job. It could be Ray, but Kim wasn't positive. "Aren't you going to tell me who you are?"

"In time," he said. "When I'm sure you're interested—or you've used up your fifteen remaining questions. Whichever comes first."

"I'm very curious right now," Kim responded coyly.

"Not curious enough," came the reply. "I'll call you next week. Bye." Kim heard the phone click off before removing it from her ear.

A moment later her shock at his reply faded, and she slammed her fists on the table. She hated it when people played games with her! Yet the boy was right. She was growing more intrigued with him with each passing second. She had to find out who he was!

Kim could think about nothing but the mystery boy during most of her show. But as the last quarter hour began to pass, she remembered another boy. From then on she kept a watchful eye on the large, round clock in front of her, mentally counting down the seconds marked off by the sweep of the bright red second hand. Three-twenty. Five minutes late already. She turned her gaze to the second microphone Rodney had set up and to the empty seat behind it. Buddy was nowhere in sight.

In a way Kim wasn't surprised. It was just like a politician to break a promise. She wasn't sure, though, whether he never intended to show up or if he'd decided to chicken out at the last minute.

Shaking her head, she handed Rodney another record. If Buddy didn't show, she could finish her program with the three singles she'd brought along with her.

Three-twenty-one. Kim was surprised at how disappointed she'd begun to feel. Until then she hadn't realized just how much she had been looking forward to the challenge of Buddy's visit. Many times during the day she had imagined the scene in her head: her introduction of Buddy in which she painted him in glowing terms, followed by his own gracious thanks for her allowing him the time to air his views. After he finished, she imagined the two of them exchanging a few pleasant comments and maybe even Buddy introducing the final song of the program.

Kim had been pleased with the way things went in her daydream, where she'd acted like a real professional. In years to come, she'd probably have to interview lots of people she didn't care for, and she figured this was as good a time as any to start. It was a shame she wouldn't get the opportunity to do it for real.

Or maybe she would. Rodney was segueing into the new song when she heard the door open behind her. There was Buddy, looking as if he'd just finished running a marathon. His face was flushed, and a few strands of his blond hair drooped over his damp forehead. He held several sheets of paper in his hand. "Am I too late?" he panted.

"Don't you know to knock first?" Kim chided him. "For all you know, I could have been talking, and your barging in would have been heard all over Laurence."

"Doesn't the red light outside go on when you're talking? I saw it was off, so I thought it was all right to come in."

Kim nodded. "Come on over here. I've got a chair waiting for you."

Buddy sat down. "See, I know something about radio, too."

"Good," Kim said. "I'm looking forward to watching you play deejay."

Buddy blanched. "B-but I planned to just give this speech."

"Forget the speech. We'll just sit and chat," Kim said, yanking the papers out of Buddy's hand and throwing them on the floor. "When the record's over, I'll introduce you. But make it short. We've got only six minutes left." Just then Rodney held up his hand, letting her know the record was ending. "Here we go," she whispered just before Rodney flipped the switch that opened up her mike.

"That was Spandau Ballet on K-LAU. This is Kim Belding, and I've got a special treat for you. In our studio right now we have an important guest, someone who really needs no introduction, especially to regular listeners of this show. Now, Buddy Forward, I know you think I've been a little hard on you lately, but it's all been in fun, right, Buddy?"

Buddy didn't know how to respond. He had

expected a formal introduction from Kim and then the opportunity to read the short speech he'd brought with him. He hadn't counted on Kim's conversational lead-in or having to do without material he'd prepared. Faced with the sudden change in plans, Buddy did the only thing he could.

Freeze.

"Buddy seems to be having some problems getting through. So, Buddy, what brings you to K-LAU this afternoon?"

Buddy looked down at the mike and automatically drew away as if he'd seen a serpent. He tried to make his mouth work, but nothing came out.

Immediately Kim realized what was happening. She'd seen it before in her radio production class—kids who were so intimidated by the microphone that they were struck speechless. But she had never expected this to happen with such an experienced speaker as Buddy. Without further hesitation she tried to cover Buddy's silence. "We seem to be having some difficulty with our equipment, and I understand Buddy's voice can't be heard out there. We'll try to get it fixed as soon as possible. In the meantime here's a classic cut from Fear."

As soon as her mike was off, Kim couldn't resist pointing out the irony. "Some choice of group, huh?" she said, turning to face him.

But she regretted the words as soon as they

came out. Buddy didn't see any humor in the situation. Tight-lipped and obviously embarrassed, he rose from the chair and stormed out of the room, banging the door shut behind him.

Rodney called out, "You want me to play 'Big Shot' by Billy Joel?"

Kim chuckled to herself. "I don't think that'll be necessary. Buddy's done more to embarrass himself than anything I could ever do."

On the way to her locker the following Monday morning, Kim spotted Buddy huddled in a small circle with Heather and two of their friends, Scott Fridell and Frannie Yarrow. Ordinarily Kim wouldn't have given them a second thought—there was nothing unusual about this group getting together for a morning chat. But that morning was different. Kim had drifted close enough to catch part of the conversation. Buddy had been talking as Kim approached them, and she heard him say her name. That was followed by a snort of disgust from Heather, who said, "What a witch!"

Kim felt she had to defend herself, even if she was eavesdropping. Pushing up the sleeves of her burgundy sweater, she ambled up to the group. "Sorry I didn't bring my hat and broomstick with me this morning, Heather," she snapped. "But they don't go with my outfit."

Heather turned to her and let out a startled gasp. Quickly she recovered from her embarrassment and flashed Kim an artificial smile. "Oh, good morning, Kim," she said. The sarcasm in her voice was obvious. "Is there anything I can do for you?"

"Yes, I'd like to know why you and your friends seem to enjoy putting me down."

The look in Heather's green eyes was one of pure innocence. "I would never do anything like that," she declared. "Why, I was just telling Buddy what a shame it was those technical problems prevented him from going on your show last Friday. I was really looking forward to listening to him. In fact, I forced myself to sit through your whole show waiting."

"I'm sure it must have been torture for you. I'm so sorry you were disappointed." She turned to Buddy, who was now leaning against a locker, looking unusually uncomfortable. "Why, I was incredibly disappointed myself. Buddy here has the potential to be a great radio star. It would have been a fabulously entertaining segment."

"Oh, cut it out, Kim," Heather said, her voice hardening. "You don't really expect me to believe that. We all know you cooked up that equipment failure excuse to keep him off the air. Right, Buddy?"

Kim was furious. She felt as if Buddy had stabbed her in the back. She'd done the decent thing, trying her best to make it sound as if Buddy hadn't choked up, and she thought she'd done a pretty good job of it. She'd played the air check as soon as she got off, and although it sounded confusing, an impartial listener would have had no reason to doubt her equipment failure excuse. Imagine Buddy telling everyone she was the reason behind his no-show appearance. He was even more of a worm than she'd thought! "Why, you—" She glared at Buddy with cold, accusing eyes.

"Heather . . ." Buddy turned sheepishly to his friend. His tone was apologetic.

"Look, Buddy," Heather explained, "I know you're too polite to knock Kim, but we both know she'd do anything to keep people like us off *her* station."

"It's not my station," Kim said. "It's the school's. And just for the record, my offer to Buddy still holds. He's welcome to come on my show whenever he wants. *If* he wants."

"I'll believe that when I hear it," Heather said. "In the meantime, I have better things to do than waste my time talking to you." She marched down the hall, the heavy sound of her boot heels causing everyone to turn and notice her.

"Uh, see you, Kim," Scott and Frannie said. They walked off, leaving Kim standing opposite a troubled-looking Buddy.

"Don't run away," he said, almost pleading with her. "I've got to explain something."

Kim snorted contemptuously. "Hasn't Heather said it all? Or do you still have more lies to throw at me?"

"No, it's not like that." Buddy sounded so shaken and troubled, Kim felt she had to listen if for no other reason than curiosity. "I don't know where Heather got those ideas about the show. I want to apologize for what she said. I know you tried to cover up for me—and I'm really grateful."

"Thanks."

"I mean it, Kim." Buddy showed a vulnerability Kim had never seen before. "I know you're not going to believe this, but every time I step in front of a microphone I get the shakes, and my throat closes up."

If Kim hadn't seen what had happened, she never would have believed Buddy. He was always calm in front of a group. She was confused. "What about all those speeches you give at assemblies?"

"You may never have noticed, but they're always written down, word for word. If I had to speak on my own, I'd die. I thought I'd be all right going on the radio, but as soon as I saw that mike, I froze. But you don't know how much I appreciate your covering for me." He chuckled. "I guess a lot of people would go wild if they knew I couldn't do something as simple as talk in front of a mike."

"How do you know I won't tell? I'd think I'd be the last person in the world you'd admit that to."

Buddy grew serious. "I may be crazy, but I trust you, Kim. I think you have more integrity than to blab something said in confidence."

Kim was surprised to hear Buddy admit this.

He seemed to be much more sensitive than Heather. "Hey, I appreciate that, Buddy. But for the record, I think you have an unreasonable fear of microphones."

"I think it's pretty unreasonable, too. But there's nothing I can do about it."

"I'm surprised a really positive guy like you hasn't tried to work this out. All it takes is some practice. Lots of people get spooked by mikes. If I were you, I'd ask Mr. Block if you could borrow one to practice talking into. Maybe he'd even let you use one of the studios when it's not busy."

"What would I do?"

Kim shrugged her shoulders. "Talking into a microphone's really not so different from talking to a friend. After a while you get used to it. All it takes is practice."

Buddy seemed to be considering her suggestion seriously. "I suppose it wouldn't hurt," he said. "Thanks, Kim, I may try that." Almost as an afterthought he added, "You know, you're not really such a bad girl after all. I think there may be some humanity underneath all your sarcasm."

You'll never find out, Buddy boy, Kim said to herself.

Chapter Five

The following afternoon Kim dawdled in the hall after her last class. It was uncharacteristic for her to do it, but getting mystery calls was pretty out of the ordinary as well. Her caller had challenged her to show him she was interested; now she was going to take him up on the offer.

So there she was waiting for Ray to walk up to his locker. She'd gone to see him play that weekend, but he'd been so wrapped up in his music and the excitement of the crowd that he hardly noticed her, although she did think she saw him wink at her a few times. He hadn't said a word to her during class, either, and she took that as a sign that she had to be more aggressive with him.

"Uh, how're you doing, Ray?" she asked, approaching him as he spun the dial on his combination lock.

She practically melted on the spot when he

45

turned and flashed her a toothy smile. "Better and better, Kim. What's up?"

"I heard you the other night at Grandma's."

"I know, I saw you. I'm glad you came."

That made Kim smile. "You guys were really tight. I liked it a lot."

"Thanks." Ray's smile grew wider.

"As you know, I play a lot of new music on my show, and I was wondering if you had a tape you wanted me to play."

"You'd do that for me?" Ray tried to sound as if it were no big deal, but his eyes betrayed his excitement. "I—uh think we've got a cut or two that'd sound good enough for the radio."

"I'm sure you've got more than that. By the way, when's your next gig?"

Ray continued to hunt through the pile of books and crumpled-up papers in his locker. "You got me there. Larry quit Sunday night." He looked out at her. "Say, you know any good drummers?"

Kim shook her head. "But I'll keep my ears open for you," she told him.

"You're terrific," Ray said, slamming his locker. "And I'll get that tape to you as soon as I can." He turned and joined the stream of students heading toward the side exit.

Kim started to replay the conversation in her head, especially the part where he said she was terrific. Suddenly she remembered she was expected elsewhere.

*   *   *

Red-faced from a quick run through the halls, Kim entered the radio station complex for the monthly staff meeting. These gatherings were mandatory for all station personnel. It was here that the faculty adviser, Mr. Block, kept everyone up to date on developments concerning the station, gave his critiques of the programming, and settled any conflicts that might have arisen during the previous month.

A soft-spoken man in his early fifties, Mr. Block was no fan of rock music, but he earned the admiration of the station staff by respecting their right to plan their own programming. He interfered in day-to-day programming decisions as little as possible, offering his input only when asked.

Mr. Block was sitting on one of the built-in desks in the front room, his left leg dangling beneath him as he poured over some papers in a manila folder. He didn't look happy, but that wasn't unusual; his lips turned down naturally, and even when he smiled, his mouth barely broke above the horizontal.

But that day Kim found his expression a cause for worry. As she pulled up a chair a horrible thought flashed through her head—perhaps Buddy was still mad and had complained about her to Mr. Block. Quickly she mounted a defense in her head, just in case, repeating to herself everything she'd said to Buddy the other day.

"Hey, Kim, glad you could make it." A voice interrupted her thoughts. "I was beginning to think you'd forgotten about us."

"I did what I felt was right," she blurted out, looking up. It was Vic. Kim gulped. "Oh, hi, Vic. I—I had to really hurry to get here—you know, old Mrs. Schroeder again. I swear the woman goes crazy if she doesn't finish her entire lesson plan on time." Somehow the thought of telling an old boyfriend about a new one just didn't seem right to her.

"I told you, you should have taken Spanish." Vic smiled impishly. "We could have been in class together."

"Then it's a good thing I didn't take Spanish," Kim answered, smiling in response. She was trying to keep their relationship where it belonged—in the past.

Vic nodded. "By the way, I caught your show Friday. I liked the way you recovered after Buddy punked out. You handled it just like a pro."

"Well, you've always told me that dead air is a deejay's worst enemy. Thanks for noticing."

"What happened with that guy, anyway? Couldn't he talk without Heather there to prompt him?"

Kim almost answered yes but stopped herself. "Uh, like I said on the air, it was equipment trouble," she said, honor-bound not to betray Buddy's secret.

Vic chose not to probe further. "Whatever it is,

48

I think your show's getting better all the time. I never miss it."

Kim smiled. "Flattery will get you everywhere."

Vic moved closer and put his arm around her shoulder. "Will it get me a date tonight?"

Kim sighed as she removed his arm. "You know that's over, Vic."

He shrugged helplessly as he rose. "I know," he said. "But you can't knock a guy for trying." He walked away slowly.

Kim turned away from Vic and glanced at the others crammed into the small room. Staffers she hardly ever saw seemed to come out of the woodwork to attend these meetings. People like Sean Englund, who was sitting cross-legged on a corner chair, trying hard to look invisible, and the Grote twins, who otherwise only showed up to do their heavy metal show on Tuesdays. Sitting right next to them was Lisa, who waved hello to Kim as their eyes made contact.

Mr. Block rapped a wooden ruler on the desk. "Take your seats, everyone." As the staffers found their way to the chairs scattered around the room, Mr. Block rose from the desk and paced nervously in the back corner. The manila folder was tucked under his right arm. "Thank you for coming today. I'll try to make this meeting as brief as possible."

That's what he always says, Kim thought ruefully, But sometimes the meetings tended to drag out for as long as an hour.

"As you know, K-LAU was founded in 1957 by some enterprising members of the Laurence Board of Education, who felt that students like you should have the opportunity to learn about radio through hands-on experience. You may not realize this, but it was a pioneering move on their part. Over the years they were able to get the support of companies who donated equipment and money to keep the station going."

Mr. Block stopped pacing and faced the group. "Back in those days it was relatively easy. More families were sending their children to school. The tax base was large, and the taxes themselves were low. No one questioned anything that was being done for education."

Vic stood up. "Mr. Block, we're all finding this history lesson very informative, but what does this have to do with us?"

Mr. Block slammed the folder down on the desk. "Everything, Mr. Pastore," he said. "Last night the school board voted to set up a committee to study the feasibility of keeping this radio station on the air. That's their way of saying that your days here may be numbered. I'm afraid it doesn't look good. There were several people on the board who want the station cut from next year's budget. If they did that, K-LAU would have to shut down."

There was a moment of silence while everyone in the room digested the news. Then in a rush twenty-five voices shouted their disapproval.

"No! They can't do that!" "They have no right!"
"It's not fair!"

"Quiet!" Mr. Block's voice rose above the din.
The room grew silent again. "I know it's not fair,
and I'm as upset about it as you are. I argued
with the board, but they said money is tight and
they are going to have to make choices. It was—"

"How come we're just finding out about this
now?" Kim asked angrily. "You should have let
us know earlier. We could have gone to that
meeting—done something."

"That's uncalled for, Miss Belding," Mr. Block
said harshly. "I had no idea this was on the
board's mind. As far as I knew, K-LAU was
exempt from budgetary considerations—it
always has been. But frankly, there are some
people on the board who don't like the direction
the programming has taken in recent years, and
that's causing them to take another look."

"They have no right to do that," Lisa cried out.
"The board doesn't run the station. We do!"

"I know, Miss Vonder. I think their attitude is
as unreasonable as you do. But they do control
the funds for the station."

"Don't they realize how many people like what
we do?" Kim pleaded. "Don't we count for anything?"

"I'm sure they'll take your feelings into consideration. As I said, they're going to study the situation. They haven't made any decisions yet. I'm

just warning you about what may happen in the future."

"Well, I don't like it," Kim continued.

"None of us do," Mr. Block said gently. "But we're going to have to make the best of it."

"It doesn't look good," said Bryce Alcott, another deejay. "Are we supposed to change the format?"

"And give in to them?" Kim's voice was full of defiance. "I'm not going to change my program."

"I don't think you should, either," Mr. Block replied. "All the board sees is a simple case of economics. The station costs more to operate than they're willing to spend."

Kim jumped up again. "I don't know about anyone else, but I'm not going to let this happen. I'm going to talk to Ms. O'Malley right now!"

"Miss Belding, wait!" Mr. Block shouted as she ran out the door. Kim could hear him even as she tore down the stairs toward the first floor administration office. But she didn't care. No one was going to stop her.

Kim heard the phone ringing down the hall from her bedroom, but she didn't feel like answering it. After everything that had happened that day, she felt she deserved some time to wallow in self-pity. The meeting with Ms. O'Malley had been a giant disaster. Right afterward Kim had come home and gone into her room. She had started to play her records in alphabetical order and decided she wasn't coming out until she'd heard the final cut on a Z.Z. Top album.

"Kim!" Her ten-year-old-sister Kate was pounding on the door. "Telephone for you!"

"Tell whoever it is I died," she yelled back.

"He says it's important."

He? The only 'he' that crossed Kim's mind was Ray. Maybe he wanted to come over that night to give her his tape. She decided to take the call after all. Turning down the stereo she said, "I'll be right out."

Kim ran a hand through her hair as she hurried to the phone. "Hello," she said sweetly.

It was Vic. "How'd it go with the big O?"

"Oh, hi, Vic," she said, deflating rapidly. "The meeting was a total waste. She's not on our side at all—though I suppose I shouldn't have found that too surprising. Buddy and Heather are her pet students. All she did was show me numbers and graphs and statistic me to death with reasons why she thinks it would make economic sense to shut the station down. I don't care how their numbers add up—it still doesn't make any sense to me." Kim's frustration came bubbling to the surface again. She started to walk down the hall with the phone. "I feel so helpless. The station is my life. I don't know what I'm going to do without it."

"We haven't lost it yet."

"Mr. Block made it sound as if it was only a matter of time."

"*Only* if we don't fight back. Mr. Block said something worth remembering. This station's been around for a long, long time. The students may come and go, but it's got deep roots in this town. The signal covers the entire town. A lot of grown-ups listen to Lisa's news and to those educational programs at night. What if we could get the town to rally behind the station? It's *their* tax dollars we're talking about. And what if we could raise money in the community and at school as a show of support?"

"But what if they want the station to die? Ms. O'Malley told me they could buy an awful lot of textbooks with the money they're now putting into the station."

"I can't believe you of all people believe that argument. What about the new uniforms the football team got this year? I'm sure the money they spent on those could have bought a ton of books. Or what about the pay increases the board voted itself?"

Kim felt her spirits returning. "I see what you mean, Vic. And you think that if we can prove the need for the station, the board might reconsider?"

"Isn't it worth a shot?"

"We'd better get started right away!" Kim exclaimed. "We've got to come up with a strategy, Vic. Get everyone working in a hurry."

"We already have. After you left the meeting, we decided to form a Save K-LAU committee. Our first meetings's tomorrow afternoon."

"Great! I'll be there."

"You'd better be. You're the chairperson."

"I'm what?" Kim's voice rose in surprise.

"I appointed you—and nobody objected."

"You could have asked me first. Why me?"

"Why not? I've got my hands full running the station. And who else around here is more devoted to K-LAU than you?"

"Well—" Kim was hard pressed to come up with a better answer to that question. "But it's an awfully big responsibility."

"You can handle it," Vic said confidently. "Besides, the decision's already been made. I'd sure hate to have to waste another day or two looking around for someone else to do the job."

Kim didn't like the way Vic took charge. It was one of the main reasons she'd broken up with him. But she didn't feel like quibbling now—the radio station was too important. She owed it to herself and the station to try to rise to the challenge. "You can count on me," she told him.

"Good," he said. "I want you to present your plan at tomorrow's meeting."

"What plan?"

"Your ideas on how we can mobilize support for the station."

"By tomorrow afternoon?" Kim shrieked. "I've got math homework to do."

"That's never seemed to stop you before."

"Still, you're not giving me very much time."

"We don't *have* very much time," Vic retorted. "Mr. Block seems to think we've got to build up support for the station before the next board meeting. That gives us only a month. So I suggest you start spinning that little brain of yours right now."

"OK," Kim said. "I'll try my best."

"I'll see what I can come up with in the meantime myself," Vic said. "And, Kim, we're going to make it work. We really are."

"You bet we are," Kim agreed.

Chapter Six

As soon as Kim got off the phone with Vic, she hurried back to her room and started listing money-making ideas. If the students and community could raise money for the station, the board would have to listen and continue their support. It made her feel much better to be doing something; moping around really didn't suit her. In less than fifteen minutes she'd covered ten pages of a legal-sized pad with ideas, descriptions, and sketches detailing her plans to raise money. Some, like her notion to charge listeners for their song requests, were wildly impractical, but if only half of them were actually put into action, she was sure it would be enough to fund the station for a long time.

She decided to start her fund-raising program at once. Bending down to the bottom drawer in her dresser, she took out a twenty-dollar bill from the coffee can in which she'd been saving money for a new cassette deck. The first donation to the Save K-LAU Fund. It wasn't much, she knew, but she had to start somewhere.

The following morning she breezed happily into her radio production class and placed twenty-one dollars and twenty-five cents on Mr. Block's desk.

The teacher eyed Kim with puzzlement. "What's this all about?"

"It's the beginning of the Save K-LAU Fund," she proclaimed proudly. "The first donations from the Belding family—from my sister Kate and me."

"That's very generous of you. But you know there are no guarantees—" Mr. Block started.

"We're not asking for any—only a chance," Kim declared. "And I hope you're willing to help us."

"I'll do what I can," he said. "As I told you yesterday, I believe the board is wrong. They're looking only at the short-term effects of taking K-LAU off the air. I hope our drive will make them understand."

Kim could see new worry lines etched on Mr. Block's forehead. She suddenly realized that if the station was lost, the faculty adviser might be out of a job. "You don't think they'll want to scrap the entire broadcasting program, too, do you? They can't—can they?"

"Well—they're still committed to the program for the time being." Mr. Block heaved a pessimistic sigh and added, "But that's what they always told me about the station, too."

"We're going to make the board see how wrong they are," she said. "I've come up with some ideas that ought to work."

Mr. Block picked up the money from the desk and handed it back to Kim. "You'd better hold on to this for now. We'll talk more about those issues at the meeting."

"Thanks, Mr. Block. And I'm sorry if I said anything to hurt your feelings yesterday."

"Apology accepted, Miss Belding."

Even though there'd been very little time to spread the word, a horde of students squeezed into the KLAU offices that afternoon. Kim counted forty when she arrived, and still more were coming into the room. She was pleased about the large turnout. The entire staff was there, as well as some kids from Kim's radio production class and a few others who'd heard about the station's problems during the day.

Kim pushed her way through the noisy crowd to join Vic, Lisa, and Kevin Montague, the chief engineer, at the front of the room. Barely audible in the background was a speaker playing the KLAU broadcast. Kim could hear her own voice coming from the program she'd recorded during lunch so she could attend the meeting.

Vic smiled at Kim and gave her a thumbs-up

sign, which she returned. She looked at the crowd of expectant kids. She'd thought up several more projects during the day and had a massive pile of papers to wade through. But she wished she were more organized.

"Hey, let's get started," Vic said, banging on the wall to get everyone's attention. All eyes focused on the gangly boy as the room quieted down. "Thanks for coming, everybody. I'm glad to see you're all concerned about saving K-LAU. We don't have much time, but with your help we can make the difference and keep this station *on* the air—where it belongs!"

A spontaneous cheer erupted.

"Hey, that's terrific. That's the spirit we need. I've asked Kim"—he nodded in her direction—"to come up with some ideas to raise money and the consciousness of this town. Kim, what do you have for us?"

Kim stood up and faced the crowd without any trace of the nervousness she usually felt when giving oral presentations in class. "There are a lot of things we can do to save K-LAU," Kim began. "Some are ambitious and are going to take a lot of work on your part." Some of the people in front of her started to groan, so she added quickly, "But some—like talking about the station's situation on your shows, for example—are easy. I've typed up copies of a petition that I want everyone here to sign and then circulate. Then I think we ought to start fund-raising drives within the school and within the Laurence business community, have a fund-raising auction or raffle, and more self-promotion on all K-LAU radio programs."

Kim went on to suggest other ideas, including selling K-LAU T-shirts, buttons, and bumper stickers, having a bake sale, publicizing the cause in the Laurence *Tribune* and on KDEH, Laurence's only other radio station, and promoting a pep rally at the school. "I realize that all these things may not add up to enough money to keep K-LAU on the air, but our hope is that if we can prove how much support this station has, then—and only then—the school board might be pressured into realizing what a terrible mistake it would be to vote us out of existence. All of you can help us meet this goal. Every signature on every petition you carry around, every phone call you make will help. Even if you can only buy a raffle ticket, you'll be showing the school board that you really care."

The entire room applauded when Kim was finished speaking. "Thanks," she whispered over the din, grateful that she wasn't in this alone.

"I'm running the story on the five o'clock news," Lisa told her.

"Great," Kim said.

"I already did some student-in-the-halls interviews," Lisa said. "Lots of them are behind us."

Just then Vic rapped the wall again. "Let's quiet down here. Kim's come up with some great ideas, but the floor's open to anyone else. Comments? Suggestions?"

"Let's put posters around school," Rodney suggested.

"Good," Kim said.

"We should all go en masse and complain at the next board meeting," Lisa declared.

"That's already taken care of," Mr. Block pointed out. "Vic and I will be representing the station at the next meeting. But I believe it's very important to get as many students involved in other activities as possible. I think Kim's suggestion of a rally is a wonderful idea."

"Yeah, you're right," Vic said. "And I've been thinking of some ways we can raise money, too. I think we ought to sponsor a dance."

"Great idea, Vic," Kim said. Several others also voiced their approval.

"Wait, there's more," Vic continued. "We'd make money by charging admission, but we could raise even more by tying it in with a contest. And I think I've got just the right ticket. A win-a-date-with-one-of-our-deejays contest."

"How would that work?" Kevin asked,

"Simple. We'd give away a grand prize—a date with one of our most popular personalities. Lots of radio stations do it all the time. We'd build up a lot of excitement on all the programs. The winner would be the big guest of honor at the dance, and if we charge a dollar for each entry, I'd bet we'd get lots of takers. In any event, the publicity we'd get could be enormous."

"Great gimmick, Vic," said Kim. "But who's the lucky deejay going to be?"

A sly grin began to cross Vic's face. "You, of course."

"Oh, no!" she cried, shaking her head violently.

"I thought you thought it was a cute idea."

"Not when it's me you're selling to the highest bidder," she retorted angrily, embarrassed to be put in this position in front of a roomful of people.

"You've got it wrong, Kim. I don't want to auction you off. This is an equal opportunity contest. Anyone with a dollar's got a chance. Hey, the more I think about it, the more I like it. What do you think, Mr. Block?"

The faculty adviser was caught off guard. "Well," he said slowly, "it *is* a rather unorthodox idea—"

"So is a lot of what we do around K-LAU. That's what makes us so special," Vic said. The crowd began to cheer. Fueled by their support he went on, "And Kim is one of our most popular deejays. I'll bet a lot of people in this town would like to take her to the dance."

"I think it's up to Kim," Mr. Block said. "If she doesn't want to do it, I don't think—"

"I bet there are at least a hundred guys out

there who would enter the contest," Vic insisted. Setting his dark, pleading gaze on her, he asked, "Are you willing to let that much money go down the drain, money that could help keep us on the air?"

"You're not being fair, Vic," Kim said through clenched teeth.

Vic couldn't be stopped now. "Aren't you willing to sacrifice *just one night* of your life for K-LAU? It seems to me a small price to pay for all this station has done for you. Besides, you might even get a boyfriend out of the deal. I'll bet there are lots of girls who'd love to be in your shoes right now."

"That shows you how much you know about girls," Kim retorted. "I'd have to be crazy to do something like this. Right, Lisa?" She turned to her friend for support.

"I don't know, Kim. It sounds kind of exciting. If I were you, I'd be flattered."

Vic's smug expression bothered Kim even more than Lisa's remarks. "See, Kim?" he said. "Maybe I'm right after all. You owe it to the station to find out."

Kim didn't like the idea of being anyone's prize. But the station did mean everything to her, and if it could help the station . . .

"Come on, Kim," urged Kevin.

"Oh, all right." Kim gave in reluctantly. "But only because it's for the station."

"You won't regret it, Kim," Vic said, reaching over to squeeze her shoulders as the crowd started cheering and whistling. "Believe me, you won't."

Chapter Seven

There was no time to waste. After the meeting broke up, Kim went to the production studio with Rodney to record some on-air promotions for the station. Her messages were short and to the point. "K-LAU is you," she told her listeners, "and without your support it's going to die. Please help keep K-LAU on the air." And "Be on the right side of the LAU. Help support K-LAU."

"Good job," Rodney said after they finished.

"A good start, perhaps, I've only just begun to fight," Kim vowed. "By the end of this week, you can bet that everyone in Laurence is going to know about us."

Kim was as good as her word. Although she couldn't take all the credit for spreading the news about the station, it quickly became the hottest issue both around the school and around the town. Two days after their meeting, the Laurence *Tribune* carried a big article, quoting Vic extensively on the students' drive to save their station. Kim wasn't interviewed for the article, but she was happy about the way it came out. The reporter had taken their campaign seriously and had let Vic present his arguments for keeping KLAU on the air. Vic stressed the point that the educational programs and nightly newscasts presented on the station were invaluable to the community.

On the day she started taking her petitions around town, Kim was dressed in her usual style: a short skirt, tights, a checkered T-shirt, and long, dangling earrings. She was full of enthusiasm as she walked into her first store, the Gift Cart, at the far end of a small shopping center near the high school. Stepping gingerly around the displays of crystal and fine china in the otherwise empty store, she approached the shop's owner, a plump and neatly dressed gray-haired woman. "Excuse me," Kim said politely. "I'm from K-LAU—"

"What's that?" the woman asked. She eyed Kim strangely.

"K-LAU. The Laurence High radio station. I was wondering if you would like to help us save it." She held out a clipboard containing her petition.

"Save it from what?" the woman wanted to know.

"The school board," Kim said. "They're considering closing us down, and we're trying to fight them. Will you help us?"

"If the school board doesn't like you, I don't see why I should, either," the woman responded tartly. "I'm sure the board has a very good reason for its actions." She continued to look at Kim contemptuously.

Kim let the woman's remarks slide past her. Now was no time to get sensitive to criticism. She plugged on in her defense of the station. "We've been providing a service to the people of Laurence for over a generation," she went on. "We think the school board's attitude is wrong and not in the best interests of the town."

"You actually operate the station?"

"We do all the programming and newscasts. We operate under all the rules of the Federal Communications Commission, just like any other radio station."

"Let me be frank," the woman said. "I'm all for education, but with kids dressed in crazy outfits like yours"—she pointed at Kim—"no wonder education's in trouble today."

Kim picked up the clipboard and shoved it under her arm, then turned on her heel and walked away briskly. *She has some nerve to criticize my clothing*, Kim thought angrily. She was almost out the door when she remembered something. "I just want you to know that if

K-LAU goes off the air, so will all of its educational programs. Why, last year alone over twenty people got their high-school diplomas from taking those on-the-air courses."

The woman looked up, interested. "Really? Now that's something worth saving."

Kim walked back slowly. "So will you sign, please?" she asked.

"I'm still not sure—I'll have to think about it." The woman hesitated. "Let me take one of those petitions and come back and see me in a couple of days."

"My pleasure," Kim said, taking one of the sheets off her clipboard.

"But first see if you can do something about those awful clothes."

Fortunately for Kim not everyone in the shopping center was such a hard sell. She had far less trouble getting signatures from several other store owners. Carl of Carl's Records and Video was particularly enthusiastic, even offering to donate some records to the station's music library. "Leave a copy of the petition here, too. I'll make sure all my customers sign," he promised Kim. She even got several signatures from some of them before leaving the store.

The counter boy at the coffee shop next door also agreed to post a petition by his cash register, as did the young woman at the beauty salon, whose leopard-print shirt was wilder than any-thing in Kim's wardrobe. Kim got some resistance from the owner of the hardware store, who turned out to be the younger brother of a member of the school board and didn't want to cause any family friction.

Nevertheless, Kim was still in good spirits as she approached her last stop, the Shop Mart supermarket. She hoped to get permission from the store manager to hold future fund-raising efforts outside the store's busy entrance. But as she neared the door, she found her way blocked by a long stack of shopping carts and the stock boy, who was guiding them into the market. "Well, look who it is!" she said. "Buddy Forward. The student leader is king of the shopping carts, too. How do you do it?"

"Hi, Kim," Buddy said cheerfully. "Say, I heard about the station. Tough break."

"You don't have to say it as though it was the best thing since automatic doors." She followed Buddy into the store.

"It's not exactly a major tragedy, either," he told her as he leaned against one of the carts.

"Oh, come on, Buddy," Kim said, her exasperation rising. "I know we've had our differences, but this is no laughing matter."

"Who's laughing? I just agree with the board that a study should be made. The station costs the school a lot of money."

"And it's money well spent. How can you support them? This issue concerns you, too," Kim noted.

"Yeah, I know. I'm Mr. Radio Personality himself," Buddy said with a laugh. He added, "I wanted to say it before you did."

Kim threw her petitions down on top of one of the carts. "Oh, I see. Just because you've got a bad case of the shakes, you'd be happy to see the station off the air? I think that's awfully self-centered of you."

"That has nothing to do with it. I'd feel badly if K-LAU had to go off the air. But we're talking realities here, Kim. The radio station eats up a lot of the school's budget. It's a luxury Laurence may not be able to afford anymore."

"If you buy the argument that it *is* a luxury—which I don't. I say the board can't afford to abandon us now. Who's to say that tomorrow they might not decide the Science Club costs too much to fund? Or the Drama Club? Or the football team?"

"The football team?" Buddy asked.

"No, not the football team." Kim managed a smile. "They'd never get rid of *that.* But they might draw the line at the student council. Do you see what I mean?" she asked, looking closely at Buddy for a sign that said he did. "All of these activities are what help make Laurence valuable. If you take one away, it sets a precedent for taking them all away. We have to make a stand now, before the board makes its final decision."

"And how do you propose to change their minds?"

"With this, for starters." She held out her petition. "I've already gotten very positive responses from a lot of people. How about you? Would you care to sign?"

Buddy read the petition. "I'll have to think about it, Kim," he said seriously. "I don't put my name on anything without thinking it out completely."

Kim was amazed at Buddy's reluctance to commit himself. "Whose side are you on?" she demanded.

"I don't see it as an us-versus-them issue," he said. "I'm on the side of what's right for everyone."

"I see." Kim pursed her lips. "I suppose you think I'm wasting my time. You'll probably go home and have a good laugh about it.

"Hey, don't sell me short, Kim. Just because I'm not rushing out to join your cause doesn't mean I think it's totally worthless. I think it's great that you have the courage of your convictions. If you're willing to fight for K-LAU, go all out for it. Prove to the board they'll have a good reason to keep you guys going."

"But don't count on you for any help."

"Not yet."

Kim perceived a glimmer of hope. "You mean

you still might support us in the future? Gee, if we could get the student council behind us . . ."

"I said I'd think about it," Buddy repeated. "I mean it, Kim. That's the best I can do for now. But I do wish you luck. And if you want, I'll even introduce you to Mr. Carnstall, the manager."

Kim appreciated the gesture. "Thanks, Buddy. If you don't watch out, I'll make a convert of you yet."

Over the next few days Kim and her committee made considerable progress. With Mr. Block's help, they got the support of a number of Laurence High's faculty members. The petition posted on the bulletin board outside the KLAU complex was filled with signatures. Kim beamed when she spotted Ray's name in large, flowing letters. She'd been so busy on the campaign that she was shocked to realize she hadn't thought about him for days. He hadn't yet revealed himself as her mystery boy, either, but Kim hadn't given up on him and looked at the signature as a sign that he was on the same side as she was.

She wished she could say as much about the dozen or so school leaders who hadn't rallied behind the station. They seemed to be united behind Heather, who took joy in the station's predicament. Heather considered the board's action as proof of every criticism she'd ever voiced about KLAU's programs and personalities.

"You're wasting your time," she called out to Kim one afternoon after Kim had stopped at the Clubhouse to pick up a petition.

Kim was glad for opportunity to spar with her rival. She marched up to the table where Heather and her friend Lindsay were sitting. Waving the petition in front of Heather's face, Kim demanded, "You call this a waste?"

"You bet I do." Heather's eyes narrowed into small slits. "The school board doesn't care about a bunch of names. For all they know, they could be forged."

"You just can't admit there may be some people around here who'd miss K-LAU, can you?" Kim countered.

"Obviously there are an awful lot who'd be happy to see it go," Heather shot back. "I'm glad the school board had the guts to take on you people."

"It's not an us-versus-them issue," Kim said, echoing the remark Buddy had thrown at her. She stopped talking and let the music playing in the background punctuate her argument. "What do you think you're listening to right now?"

"Garbage," Heather answered back, with Lindsay nodding in agreement. "I can't help it if the only place in town that makes a decent cheeseburger has no taste in music. I ignore it as best I can." She looked up at Kim and smirked. "Oh, by the way, Kim, don't miss my editorial in the next issue of the *Messenger*. You radio people have been making so much noise, I wanted to make sure that the board knows there are people at Laurence behind them one hundred percent."

"I think you're outnumbered on this one," Kim said. "There are more people supporting our fight than you think—and they're not just Laurence students. You'll see."

Kim didn't tell Heather that just then she was on her way to an appointment with Nathan Lyman, the publisher of the Laurence *Tribune*. After he'd run the article about the station, Vic had asked Kim to call Mr. Lyman and try to get his support. Kim had been surprised when he agreed to see her; she'd had the feeling that someone so important wouldn't want to be bothered with a high-school student. But he'd told her he was anxious to meet her.

The *Tribune* was located in a two-story, tan stucco building about a half mile from the Clubhouse. Mr. Lyman's office was in a corner on the first floor, just beyond the large open room where the reporters worked. Kim passed five or six people busily banging out articles. There was a portable radio on one of the desks, and as Kim grew closer, she recognized the familiar voice of Ian Strauss doing his afternoon show on KLAU.

Kim was elated. It appeared she was in friendly territory.

She didn't have to wait to see Mr. Lyman, and she was ushered into his office before she had a chance to double-check that her skirt lay right. She'd dressed as conservatively as she could, wearing a plain lavender skirt and a black sweater. She didn't want to put off the publisher the way she had the woman at the Gift Cart.

Mr. Lyman, a short, wiry man in his thirties, rose from behind the antique wooden desk and greeted her. "Welcome, Kim," he said warmly. "Have a seat right here." He motioned to one of the green leather chairs that was next to his desk. "How's the committee doing?" he asked as soon as she sat down.

Kim waited until he returned to his seat to speak. "We're working hard," she said. "We've been circulating petitions around town, appealing to our listeners over the air for support. We're organizing a fund-raising dance, too, and a contest that goes along with it." She deliberately left the details of the contest vague, not wanting to mention that she was the big prize. "After the article in your paper came out, we got a bunch of letters urging us to keep up the pressure on the board. There are lots of people in this town who don't want us to close down."

"I'm well aware of that," Mr. Lyman said, taking off his metal-rimmed glasses and dangling them off his right hand. "We've gotten a number of letters here, too." He chuckled as he reached across his desk with his other hand and grabbed a candy jar filled with chocolate-covered peanuts. "Want some?" he offered Kim. He took a handful for himself after she declined. "I'm afraid I don't get to listen to K-LAU as much as I'd like. What's your connection with the station?"

"I'm a deejay," Kim said proudly. "I'm on three days a week."

"Hmmm." The publisher rapped his glasses against his knuckles. "You must be pretty good. In my day the best deejays only got to work two shifts a week."

Kim was dumbstruck. "You mean you used to be at K-LAU?"

Mr. Lyman's blue eyes crinkled at the edges. "I was music director in 1967. We called it simply K-L-A-U back then," he remembered. "I was on every Monday and Tuesday from four to five."

"What was it like?" Kim asked.

"We played all the newest rock music we could find. Boy, I still remember all the commotion that went on the day we first played *Sgt. Pepper's Lonely Hearts Club Band*."

"The Beatles' album," Kim acknowledged. She had it somewhere in her collection at home.

Mr. Lyman shot a quick glance at the lights on his telephone. "I think I get plenty of calls now, but it's nothing compared to what went on that day. Everyone wanted to know where they could buy the album," Mr. Lyman continued. "And then there were the requests. Do you still do those?"

"All the time," Kim said. "Sometimes people ask for the same song over and over. Even if it's a song I like, I usually end up hating it."

"Nothing really changes, does it? I don't think I ever did a show where someone didn't ask for 'Light My Fire' by the Doors. I still can't stand to hear it. But enough of my ramblings. I'm sure I'm boring you."

"Not at all," Kim said, anxious to hear more.

"But that's not why you're here." He put on his glasses, then sorted through the papers on his cluttered desk. "I think you might enjoy reading this." Mr. Lyman handed Kim a galley.

Kim sat back in the chair and examined the sheet of paper. On it was an editorial voicing strong objection to the school board study. "The board fails to see the educational value of this radio station," it read in part.

Having eyes that focus only on the balance sheet, they fail to take into consideration all the people who've walked through those studio doors over the years and walked out with enough experience to land jobs in radio stations all over the country. Even those who chose not to enter broadcasting were enriched by the professional atmosphere and commitment to excellence that has been a hallmark of KLAU ever since it went on the air. Doesn't that count for anything? We think it does.

"This is going to run in tomorrow's paper," Mr. Lyman explained. "I wanted to let you know personally that you kids are not in this alone."

"You don't know how much this means," Kim said gratefully. "I don't know how to thank you."

"Just do the best job you can."

On her next show Kim featured the Beatles' *Sgt. Pepper* album. She dedicated "A Little Help from My Friends" to Mr. Lyman.

The following morning the *Tribune* editorial was displayed prominently on the KLAU bulletin board with the words, "*Read This!*" scribbled underneath it in a red grease pencil. Kim noticed it on her way into the station just before lunch period. She figured Vic had put it there. How many people would be swayed by Mr. Lyman's argument still remained to be seen, but she realized that it was the most important endorsement they'd received so far—and the campaign was only a week old.

There was another opportunity coming up for further support. At its meeting the following Tuesday, the student council was going to consider a resolution urging the school board to keep the station going. Kim was going to argue on the station's behalf. It was an endorsement she was very anxious to have.

Kim was about to enter the station when Buddy came up behind her. "What are you doing here?" she asked him.

"I just saw Vic, and he told me there was something up here I ought to see."

"He must mean this." Kim pointed to the editorial. "This just goes to show that not everyone thinks we're useless."

Buddy defended himself. "I never said you were useless." He read the editorial quickly. "You must be pleased," he said.

"I think it means a lot," Kim said. "But it'd help just as much to have the student council behind us. Are you going to support us?"

"You'll find out on Tuesday."

Kim rolled her eyes. "My, my, aren't we being coy today."

"Not at all," Buddy said. "The council is going to vote on the resolution then. It'd be presumptuous of me to predict what the rest of them are going to do."

"But what about you, Buddy? Keeping your vote a secret?"

"I haven't made up my mind yet. The arguments are strong on both sides. Uh, I'd like to stay and talk more, but I've got to run, Kim. See you around."

What is it going to take to convince that guy?

Kim wondered as she watched him leave. She didn't know the answer just then, but she knew she'd have to come up with one in time for the meeting.

Chapter Eight

"Jennifer, help me roll this out, will you?"

Kim and Jennifer were standing in the Belding garage the following Saturday morning. At their feet was a large roll of brown paper. "What is it?" Jennifer asked.

"Nothing yet. That's why I asked you to come over." Jennifer followed Kim's lead and knelt down at the opposite end of the roll. Together they unrolled about a fifteen-foot sheet of paper. "We're going to paint a sign announcing the dance. It took Mr. Block two days of arguing, but Ms. O'Malley finally gave us permission to put up a poster by the entrance to the school. I'm going to make sure no one misses it."

"It's about time. The dance *is* next Saturday. Anyway, you've called the right person. I always did get A's in penmanship."

"Don't think I didn't remember." Kim got up and grabbed the box of poster paints she'd bought the day before while making her rounds of Laurence businesses.

"I think we should write 'SAVE K-LAU' in big red letters," Jennifer said. She tucked her long brown hair into the back of her T-shirt. "How'd it go yesterday afternoon?"

"I got about a hundred and fifty more signatures out at the Plum Tree Mall," Kim said, beaming with pride. "A lot of Laurence kids, but also a lot of Laurence grads who used to listen when they went to school here. They really hate the idea of K-LAU being axed, even though they don't listen anymore."

"Say, what do you think of this?" Jennifer asked. She had drawn three-dimensional call letters that looked like lightning bolts.

Kim leaned over her friend's shoulder. "Great!" she said enthusiastically. "You'd be surprised at how many people I've met these past few days who are all for the idea of there being a student radio station. Especially when they see such a clean-cut example of today's modern teen."

"You? Clean-cut? Dressed like that?" Jennifer pointed to the striped short shorts that Kim was wearing.

"You would have died to see me yesterday. My mom's blue cable knit sweater and plaid skirt— and knee socks." Jennifer's mouth flew open. "Don't go into shock. It was a little bit of advice a woman threw at me the first day I went out. I hate to admit it, but I found out the hard way that she was right. My regular clothes have a way of scaring off older people, though once I start talking I don't think it matters what I'm wearing. There are lots of people out there for us, and if we can get some of them to start making noise, our problems will be over. Unfortunately I don't think anyone wants to get more involved than signing a petition." She looked down at the sign again. "Why don't you use the blue paint to spell out 'dance'?"

"Fine with me," Jennifer said. "Haven't you been getting a lot of interest in your win-a-date contest?"

"More than I ever would have imagined. Between the dance admission, the contest, and individual donations, we're going to end up raising lots of money. I have no idea exactly how many people have entered the contest, though. Vic won't tell me. He gets his hands on the entries as soon as they come in and hides them in a locked closet."

"Sounds like you have more fans than you thought."

"Or the station does."

"Right, Kim," Jennifer said sarcastically. "Anyone who likes the station can make a direct donation. Face it, you're hot. Gosh, it must be exciting being at the center of a contest like that."

Kim sat down on the floor. "To tell you the

truth, every time I think about it, I feel like I'm for sale or something. Which I'm not," she emphasized.

"So why are you doing it?"

"For the station. The contest is getting a lot more people interested in it. Maybe some of them are willing to help us stay around."

"Has Heather come around yet?"

"Are you kidding?" Sighing, Kim shook her head. "She's still planning on running that editorial against us."

"Traitor," Jennifer hissed.

Kim nodded. "For a smart girl she's awfully shortsighted. Just because she can't control the station is no reason to be happy to see it go."

"Don't worry about her, Kim. No one likes Heather, anyway."

"I suppose," Kim said, anxious to change the topic. "You know I got another call during my show yesterday from my phone-in boyfriend. He told me he's so sure he's going to win the contest that he's not going to tell me who he is until then. Do you know what that means, Jennifer?"

"Yeah, you're going to spend the next week driving me crazy with this guy," Jennifer said.

"I promise I'll mention him only twice a day, OK?" Kim winked. In a more serious tone she said, "What I meant was that this guy must have sent in dozens of entries! He really must be crazy about me."

"Or just plain crazy. If he likes you so much,

why does he keep putting off meeting you? He must know you're interested."

"But not interested enough, he keeps telling me," Kim noted. "Maybe the signals I've been sending Ray have been too subtle."

"So you still think it's him?"

Kim shot Jennifer a knowing glance. "It certainly makes sense to me. My mystery guy told me he's been busy lately, and I know Ray's been up to his ears auditioning new drummers for his band. I also know he's been talking up the station every chance he gets. He was really excited when I played his song on my show."

Jennifer went back to work on the sign. The two of them were quiet for a while, but Kim broke the silence when she spotted the troubled look on Jennifer's face. "What's the matter?" she asked. "Something wrong with the sign?"

"No, it's fine," her friend said. "If you really want to know, I was just thinking about Ray."

"You can't have him," Kim said defiantly. "He's mine."

"I'm not so sure," Jennifer said. "At least I'm not convinced he's your mystery man. It just doesn't add up. You have a caller who says you don't act interested enough in him. Well, from what I can see, you're bending over backward to be as friendly to Ray as you can be. He'd have to be in a coma not to know you like him. Besides, he doesn't seem like the type to play a stupid waiting game like this."

"OK, Sherlock Holmes, who do you think it is?"

"I don't know—though I agree it's got to be someone you already know. I have a feeling that you're doing something that's turning this guy off and making him think you couldn't care less about him." Jennifer started to pace the garage floor. "Let's see—who have you been acting mean to lately?"

"No one," Kim answered. "With the possible exception of Buddy Forward. And I can't believe—"

"Why not?" Jennifer interrupted, thoroughly amused by the notion of Buddy's being Kim's mystery caller.

"Because it's insane!" Kim shrieked.

Jennifer raised her hands. "Now hold on there, Kim. I think I may be on to something." She looked as if she were about to burst. "Let's just say, for argument's sake, that he likes you. Wouldn't it make sense for him to lay low and be really cool about it until he was positive that you liked him, too?"

"That's ridiculous," Kim shot back. "Buddy's never been bashful about speaking his mind before." *So long as he doesn't have to do it on the radio*, she added to herself.

"But this is different," Jennifer said, really excited now. "It'd be a daring move for him to date a girl like you. And you know what a cautious guy Buddy is. It would make sense for him

87

to take his time—especially since he's been getting nothing but mixed signals from you."

"But I haven't been sending him *any* signals!" Kim exclaimed. "Except that I want him to support K-LAU."

"That proves my point," Jennifer said. "You're on one side—and Heather's on the other. And you know the influence she has on him. Has he told you where he stands yet?"

"He says he hasn't made up his mind. But at least he doesn't see us as the enemy, the way Heather does," Kim said reflectively.

Jennifer stood back and admired her sign. "I'm finished. How does it look?"

Kim smiled. "It's terrific. Thanks, Jennifer. You're a great artist—even though you're no good at deductive reasoning. There's no way in the world you're right about Buddy. But I'm so sure Ray's my guy that I'll bet you a pizza I'm right."

"You're on!" Grinning ever so slightly, Jennifer nudged Kim. "But doesn't just a little bitty part of you want to believe it's Buddy?"

Kim picked up one of the paintbrushes and brandished it playfully near Jennifer's face. "I think it's time for me to call the asylum. That's the craziest thing I've ever heard."

On Monday morning Kim raced out of her history class as soon as the bell rang. There was no reason to take her time hoping to get in a few words with Ray as he wasn't in school that day.

It was just as well, for Kim was very busy with a feature project she was preparing on the station's behalf, one she had thought of after her meeting with Mr. Lyman. The reel of audio tape she had begun to edit during her radio production class lay securely in her canvas carryall. Kim hoped to finish it during lunch, in time to air on that evening's newscast. She scrambled through the crowded hallway, then up the stairs to the production studio.

She was so preoccupied with the project that she was halfway through threading the tape on the editing machine before she noticed Buddy Forward sitting in front of the control board.

Kim gasped. Buddy was the last person she expected to see there.

Buddy turned to her. "I didn't mean to scare you. Mr. Block told me I could come in here and use the equipment. He said there'd probably be someone around who could help me out. But he didn't say it'd be you."

"Sorry to disappoint you, Buddy," Kim said. "But I'm working on a feature for tonight's news. I don't have time to play teacher."

Buddy swiveled around in the chair. "That's OK. I understand. I don't want to keep you from what you're doing." He began to get up.

Kim surprised herself by saying, "But you can

hang around if you want. This might not take so long to finish. I'll be able to help you then."

Buddy's face brightened. "Thanks, Kim. You sure you don't mind?"

"As a matter of fact, I think I'd like you to hear this. You might find it interesting."

"How come you're doing something for the news? I thought you were a deejay."

"I don't usually do this sort of thing," she told him. "But I got this idea the other day. Mr. Lyman at the *Tribune* isn't the only adult in this town who once worked at K-LAU. There are lots of others—some prominent ones, too. I've started to interview some of them, getting them to talk about their experiences here. This is the first one that's going to air." Kim turned back to the machine and finished setting up the tape. Then she leaned over Buddy to reach the board on which she flipped a few switches and turned up the red knob underneath them.

Buddy eyed her movements with much curiosity. "What are you doing?"

"Oh, just another of the useless skills I've picked up here," she said airily. She pressed another button on the board. The tape began rolling, and she adjusted the knob to control the volume of the voice now coming out of the speaker above the control board. "I set up the tape to play through that speaker," she explained quickly. "Be quiet, this is pretty fascinating stuff."

A man's voice came through the speaker telling about the controversy that erupted the first time he played an Elvis Presley record over the air. The station was new, and the music was considered scandalous back then. Several parents even complained about their children being exposed to it. But the station weathered the storm successfully and went on to become very popular with the students at Laurence High.

Kim thought that the story was highly relevant to the station's new problems. As the former deejay spoke, Kim wondered what was going through Buddy's mind. Did he find the anecdote interesting, too? Did he see its significance?

As soon as Kim pressed the stop button, he remarked, "It sounds like a good feature, Kim."

"Thanks, Buddy."

"I never stopped to think about the history of this station. It must have really been something to start from scratch like that guy did. Who *is* this guy anyway?"

"Dr. Ronald Grabowski. He's a heart surgeon now, but back then he was K-LAU's first student manager. He had a music show and called himself Ronny. He goes on to talk more about that first year. Want to hear?"

"Sure."

"I've still got to cut out some of the pauses and tighten it up a bit, but here goes." She hit the button again, playing about a minute-long segment. It took her much longer to go through it, though, as she stopped the tape and used a white grease pencil to mark the sections she wanted to delete. With the tape still on the machine, she cut out the sections on the splicing machine attached to the tape player. Then she reassembled the tape with tiny pieces of splicing tape. The whole procedure was done with lightning speed. Kim had spliced so many pieces of tape together she thought she could do it in her sleep if she had to.

Buddy looked over her shoulder in wonder. "How do you do that so fast?"

"Practice. Want to try?"

"No," he replied a little shyly. "I'd be all thumbs."

Kim finished her splices, then attached pieces of blank white leader tape at the beginning and ending of the cuts. "Now all I have to do is record my introduction and put the whole thing on a cart. Now, as for you, what can I do to help?"

"Well, I decided to follow your suggestion about practicing speaking into a microphone. Mr. Black said I should talk as if I were having a regular conversation."

"He's right—and I'm really glad you decided to try it. Let me show you a few things." Kim slipped behind Buddy and pulled out an oblong-shaped microphone that was connected to the back of the control board by a metal arm. "Here it is. A bidirectional microphone." She cradled it in her hand. "That means I can talk through this end, and you can talk through the other." She held it out for him to touch. "Believe me, it won't bite."

Buddy stuck out his hand. "I guess it's pretty stupid to be afraid of one of these things."

"You'll get over it. Now what would you like to talk about?"

He shrugged. "I don't know. Why don't you ask me some questions? Anything you'd like."

Kim leaned against the Formica console, her hands cupping the edge. "OK," she said. "Let's start with something basic. What's your name?"

Buddy grinned self-consciously. "Buddy Forward."

"No, I mean your real name. Buddy's a nickname, right?"

"Do we really have to?"

"You said I could ask you anything." Kim's eyes opened wide. "Is this a skeleton that's hiding in your closet? Some terrible, terrible name you don't want revealed?"

Buddy's grin broadened into a laugh. "I'm not trying to hide anything, I just prefer being called Buddy. My real name is Harry Marcus Forward, Jr. But everyone's always called me Buddy."

"I can see why, Harry." Kim's nose wrinkled playfully.

Buddy reached into the back pocket of his cords for his wallet. "How much do I have to pay you to keep this quiet?"

Kim grew serious. "I won't tell anyone. I know what you mean about names. My middle name is Mildred, and I never use it."

"It's not so bad. And Kim's a pretty name."

"Why, thank you, Buddy. Spoken like a true politician."

"No, I think that's my Gemini politeness showing through."

"You're a Gemini, too? When's your birthday?"

"June fourth," Buddy said. "When's yours?"

"June seventh," said Kim. "I'm really surprised. You don't act like a Gemini. You're too stable and predictable."

"Oh, I wouldn't say that. I've been known to do something crazy every now and then. Like coming into this studio, for instance. When are we going to start practicing?"

Kim smiled mysteriously. "Didn't you know? We already are." She pointed to the mike perched over Buddy's head and then to the tape machine whose red recording light was glowing brightly.

Buddy's jaw dropped. "When did you do that?" he cried.

Kim waved her slender fingers in the air. "The hands are quicker than the eye. I started up the tape just in case you wanted proof that you could speak into a mike without going into shock. Like you said, a Gemini is capable of doing the unpredictable."

After Buddy had left, however, Kim began to

wonder just how unpredictable he was. True, Buddy's visit to the studio had been a surprise. *But it was only to practice speaking so that he can keep up his Mr. Perfect image,* she thought. *But, on the other hand, we did manage to talk to each other without getting into an argument.*

Kim sighed. Maybe Buddy wasn't so simple after all.

"Hello, you've reached the K-LAU request line."

"Kim, is that you?"

Kim blanched. She recognized the whispering, raspy voice. It was *him.* "Oh, hi. What song would you like me to dedicate to myself today?"

"You know who I am?"

"Why sound so surprised? I should know your voice by now, shouldn't I?"

He chuckled. "It's not my real voice."

"I know that." Kim sighed. "Look, Ray, I'm getting tired of playing this game. Let's get this thing out into the open, OK?"

"Ray? Who's that?"

Kim froze momentarily. When she recovered she asked hesitantly, "Isn't this Ray Rollins?"

"No."

"Are you sure?"

"Positive."

"Then who are you?"

"You'll find out soon enough."

"When?"

"When you announce the winner of your contest. I'm going to win, Kim. I've got to run now, but I'm looking forward to our date. Hope you are, too."

Kim hung up the phone more confused than ever—and more than a little disappointed that her hunch about Ray had been wrong. But if he wasn't her telephone boyfriend, then who was?

Chapter Nine

The student council meeting was just beginning when Kim arrived at the school auditorium to make her presentation. Marie Garcia, the council secretary, was reading the minutes of the previous meeting. Kim took a seat next to Lisa, who was recording the meeting for her newscast. "What have I missed?" she asked.

"Nothing but the usual nonsense," Lisa whispered.

This was the first student council meeting Kim had ever attended, and as she listened to what was going on, she was glad she'd never been bitten by the political bug. Judging by Marie's minutes, Kim decided that the last month's meeting had been pretty boring—a discussion on how much money to donate to the junior prom committee and a rather lengthy debate on who was going to write the next letter to the refugee child in South America whom the council sponsored. Kim couldn't see why Buddy hadn't simply appointed someone to do the job and saved a lot of time and hassles for everyone.

But then Buddy was an ever-changing puzzle to Kim, and she wondered if she'd ever figure out how to put together all the pieces. He acknowledged her arrival with a friendly smile and nod. His Gemini politeness, she thought. She smiled back and waited, with as much patience as she could muster, for her turn to speak.

As the meeting progressed, Kim realized what it was that made Buddy stand out among the students at Laurence. As student council president, he had a lot of power, but he didn't use it to impose his views on everyone else. He let all the representatives have their say, yet there was never any doubt that he was in control. When one of the speakers started to ramble on about the need for the council to sponsor an anti-smoking campaign, Buddy cut her off gently by naming her to head a committee to study it further.

Buddy then raced through three or four more items before he got to Kim. She was pleasantly surprised by the graciousness of his opening remarks. "Council members, we're now going to go on to a very important issue, a resolution asking the student council to support our student radio station, K-LAU. As all of you are well aware, the Laurence Board of Education is considering closing down the station because of a lack of funds. You have before you a written statement from Mrs. Litvin, the school board member chairing the committee looking into this issue. Now, I am pleased to welcome Kim Belding. Kim is one of the disc jockeys on K-LAU, and in the past week she has been working tirelessly to keep the station on the air. She is here now to present her case to us."

Buddy led the council in polite applause as Kim walked to the table set up at the front of the auditorium. His remarks had lifted her spirits considerably. He had been more than polite, and it seemed as if he were on her side.

Confidently Kim outlined the reasons why KLAU should be allowed to remain on the air. She deliberately kept her remarks short, not wanting to bore the representatives. Several times during her talk, Kim glanced at Buddy, whose eyes were warm with encouragement. *The council support would really be a boost to the station,* she thought. *Perhaps Buddy might also be persuaded to change Heather's mind about printing her editorial. . . .*

After she finished, Buddy again led the council in applause for Kim. She returned to her seat to await their vote. "Thank you, Kim," Buddy said, "for a fine presentation. The council is going to go into executive session to discuss the resolution now. I'm sorry, but all nonmembers are going to have to leave."

Silently Kim and Lisa got up and walked out of

the auditorium. As the heavy wooden doors closed behind them, Kim asked, "Do they always close their meetings?"

"Whenever they want to discuss something Buddy doesn't want on the record. Don't worry. I always find out what happens anyway." She lowered her voice. "Marie loves gossip."

"What do you think our chances are?" Kim asked.

"If all they had to go on was your speech, I'd say we'd win by a landslide. You were very persuasive. And judging by the way Buddy was looking at you, I have a feeling he may be leaning toward us, too."

"What do you mean?"

"You two don't have something going, do you?"

"Have you been talking to Jennifer?" Kim cried. "I'm glad you don't run a gossip show, or there'd be rumors flying around the whole school!"

"Sorry I asked," Lisa said. "Are you going to wait here with me till the meeting's over?"

Kim shook her head. "No, waiting around will only get me nervous. I'm going up to the station and wait for the news there."

Forty minutes later Lisa ran into the station. Her cheeks were flushed, and her index finger was poised above the play button on her cassette recorder.

A half-dozen people pounced on the news director. "What happened?" they all shouted. Kim's voice was loudest of all.

"Let me through" was all she'd say. Lisa burst down the hall to the studio where Ian was doing his show. She threw open the door to the control room, ignoring the red light that meant Ian was on the air, and pulled a cartridge out from the tape rack. Ian saw the commotion going on in there and cut himself off just as his engineer, Kevin Montague, interrupted.

"We interrupt this broadcast to bring you a bulletin from the K-LAU newsroom—"

Pulling the control microphone close to her face, she announced, "This is Lisa Vonder, K-LAU news. The Laurence High School student council has turned down a resolution in support of K-LAU's drive to remain on the air. . . ."

Kim, who'd run into the studio to hear the announcement, looked at her friend in total shock. Ian, Vic, and the others who'd gathered around her were equally stunned.

"Student council president, Buddy Forward, came out of the forty-minute-long debate over the issue and told K-LAU news—" Lisa held the cassette player against the microphone and pressed down the play button. Out into the room spilled Buddy's voice. "It was a very tough decision, but these are difficult times for all of us. We sympathize with those who have put in long hours on behalf of K-LAU, but in the end we have to agree with those on the school board who believe the radio station is a luxury the town of Laurence can no longer afford."

"That was student council president Buddy Forward on the council's decision not to support radio station K-LAU. More details upcoming on the five o'clock news. I'm Lisa Vonder."

Kevin put up a record while Lisa joined the others in the studio. "Your buddy Buddy let us down in a big way," Lisa said, looking at Kim.

"But he seemed so sympathetic," Kim wailed. "And he's not *my* Buddy!" she added emphatically.

"Sympathy isn't necessarily support," Vic pointed out. "Buddy's a politician. It's his job to appear to be all things to all people."

"But not to us," Kim said. "In the end he just didn't want to disagree with the board. Or Heather," she added bitterly.

Vic put his arm on her shoulder. "Don't take it so hard, Kim. Who needs the council, anyway? We're getting more pledges from our fund-raising drive every day, and more signatures on our petitions. We've still got a good chance."

"Wait till they see the turnout at the dance," Lisa chimed in, trying to raise her own spirits.

"That's right," Vic said. "We're making lots of money from your contest alone. We might raise enough money from these things to keep the station going even without the board's help."

"You're right, guys," Kim spoke up. "We can't

give up now. We've just got to try harder, that's all." But inside she was more furious at Buddy than she thought possible. She felt terribly betrayed.

That night Kim was putting away the pile of clothes her mother had washed for her. When she got to the gray "Renegade" T-shirt near the bottom of the stack, her eyes began to mist. Kate, who had been watching her sister clean her room, grew worried. "What's the matter, Kim?"

Kim managed a smile. "Hey, it's nothing," she said quickly, folding the shirt. Had it been only two weeks earlier when she'd laughed happily about her outcast image? It seemed like a lifetime ago.

But Kim thought it best not to dwell on the problems of the station. "I've suddenly got a wild urge to make chocolate milk shakes," she said. "Want to join me?"

"Sure, let's go," Kate said.

The girls were walking through the living room to the kitchen when the phone rang. "I'll get it," Kate shouted, running to the wall phone next to the refrigerator. A few moments later she called out, "Kim, it's for you!" Cupping her hand over the phone she added in her typical giggling whisper, "It's a boy."

"Probably Vic," Kim muttered to herself. "I'll take it in Mom and Dad's room," she told Kate.

In the privacy of her parents' bedroom, she picked up the extension. "Hello," she muttered grouchily.

"Kim? It's me, Buddy—"

Kim was shocked. What could Buddy want from her now? "I have nothing to say to you," she blurted out.

"Wait a second. I knew I was taking a chance calling you, but I felt I owed you an explanation."

"For what? Denying Laurence 'the luxury it can no longer afford'?" Kim spat out. Then she scolded herself. *Don't show him how much he's hurt you. Be strong. Be mature.* Forcing herself to be calm, Kim said softly, "You don't owe me anything, Buddy. You did what you felt was right." Kim's jaw was clenched so tight she could hardly get the words out.

"I hope you really mean that," Buddy said. "I wanted to break the news to you in person, but I couldn't find you after the meeting."

"I was at the station." She felt her composure slipping.

"I had a feeling you might be, and I started to go up there until I realized it'd be like walking into the lion's den. I know how hard you guys have been working, and you've got to be disappointed with our decision. But we really feel it was in the best interest of the school. I hope you understand that."

"Understand?" Kim cried. "Oh, sure, Buddy, I understand. I understand all too well." She could feel her face heating with the anger she could no longer suppress. "You try so hard to be all things to all people. Laurence's Mr. Politician. Everybody's friend. But it didn't work this time. When the time came to lay it on the line for me, you weren't there!"

"Kim, I never promised you anything—"

"No, you never did. But you strung me along, making me believe that it was only a matter of time before you'd stand by us." She snorted. "I suppose Heather got a good laugh out of that."

"I'm sorry you feel that way, Kim," Buddy said calmly. "But I really gave it a lot of careful thought. And for the record it was the longest discussion on any topic we've had in a long time. You've got a lot of friends on the council."

"And obviously you're not one of them!" Kim finished for him. "I don't have anything else to say to you. Goodbye, Buddy!" She slammed down the phone.

Back in her room, Kim sorted through her record collection for some tunes that would make an appropriate I-hate-Buddy medley. But before she got too far along, she stopped the project. *He'd only love the attention*, she told herself. And the last thing she wanted to do right then was make Buddy happy.

Chapter Ten

"**H**i, everybody! It's Friday, and you're listening to Laurence's number-one station, K-LAU. I'm Kim Belding, and this is 'Something Different.' At the end of the show today we'll have the event you've all been waiting for, the announcement of the winner of K-LAU's Win-a-Date contest. Stay tuned. But first, 'Who Is It?' from Talking Heads—"

As the record started, Kim took off her headphones and stared at the people hovering in and around the studio. Interest in the contest was high, and the station was unusually crowded for a Friday afternoon. Staffers were gathered in the halls and the front office, anxious for the announcement to be made. Had all the boys there entered the contest? Kim wondered.

She let her eyes wander to the huge cardboard carton in the corner of the studio. Inside that box were all the contest entries—and her date for the following night. In less than an hour, Kim would reach into that carton and pull out a name.

As if the phone call the other day hadn't been enough, Kim had gotten even more evidence that morning that the name wouldn't be Ray Rollins. She'd overheard him tell Cary Hanks in history class about the girl he was taking to the K-LAU dance. Adding insult to injury, Kim had seen him huddling close to a pretty, statuesque blond after class. It had looked like true love to Kim.

The additional audience was making her nervous now, and Rodney noticed. "Kind of like vultures waiting for the kill," he commented, talking through the intercom. "You'd think we were giving away a new car. Heck, it's only a date with you!"

"What do you mean—only me?" Kim retorted, ready to defend herself. But she stopped when she realized that Rodney was only trying to lighten her mood. "Yeah, you're right, it's no big deal. Just one date with one guy for one night. It's not like it's going to kill me."

"You might even end up with me."

Kim looked squarely at her engineer. "Rodney! Did you enter the contest, too?"

"I thought the station could use my dollar," he said.

"Terrific," she said.

"I care about the station very much." Rodney

switched back to business. "The record's ending. You want the mike?"

"No, segue into the next one. I don't feel like talking too much today."

"I think you should. It'll help you get your mind off that box."

"Have you turned into a shrink all of a sudden?" Kim exclaimed.

"Just try it and see if it works."

Kim was forced to talk because Rodney was deliberately taking his time setting up the next record. Rather than treat her audience to dead air, she said, "The next song is from a new group called Smash. They're new to us, but Smash is a smash in London, where they have three records in the top ten. Coming up is one of them from their debut album, *Smashing.*" At that moment Rodney was just taking the record out of its sleeve, so Kim continued. "Before we play it, though, I want to say a word or two about an unsung hero around here—my engineer, Rodney Hartung, who keeps this show moving and always gets my records ready to play on time." Kim was amused by the way Rodney now scrambled to get the record up. "Now, here's Smash with 'On The Edge.' "

As soon as the red light went off, Kim slumped against her chair. It had been a challenge to speak off the cuff like that. But Rodney had been right. The effort had made her take her mind off the contest.

Soon there were only five minutes left in the program, and it was time to announce the winner. Vic came into the studio, and he, Kevin, and Ian pushed the carton next to Kim's chair. With a drumroll effect in the background, Kim went on the air.

"And now we have the moment you've all been waiting for. The winner of the K-LAU Win-a-Date contest. I'm reaching into the pile of names"—she paused as she dipped her hand as far down as she could reach—"and the winner is—"

She opened the folded piece of paper quickly and read out the name. "Buddy Forward!"

Kim's mike was cut as Rodney played a tape of cheering crowds. It was just as well that her anguished scream couldn't be heard over the air. *"Buddy Forward?* I don't believe it!"

Vic moved closer and took the entry slip from her hand. "Buddy Forward," he repeated matter-of-factly. "That's what it says."

So he was my mystery boyfriend after all, Kim said to herself, still not believing it could be true. It just didn't make sense. And after what had happened at the student council meeting the other day, she could never have dreamed that Buddy had sent in an entry.

Vic saw Kim's distressed look. "So Buddy got lucky," he said. "What else can I say but congratulations, Kim? And try to have a good time."

"That's easy for you to say," she muttered, wondering what Jennifer would like on her pizza. She couldn't see herself going through with this date. Somehow she'd have to find a way to get out of it. Somehow.

"The joke's up, Buddy," Kim announced over the phone several hours later.

"Who is this?" Buddy asked.

"I'm surprised you don't recognize me. It's Kim. I just wanted to tell you I don't think it's funny, and I'm not going to go."

"Go where? What are you talking about, Kim?"

"I'm talking about our date."

Buddy nearly dropped the phone. "Did I hear you right? Did you say 'date'?"

"That's right. As in the date you won with me to the dance. It's only been a few hours since I made the announcement. Surely you haven't forgotten already."

"Wait, Kim, slow down. I really don't know what you're talking about. How did I win a date with you?"

Kim was confused now. "The K-LAU contest. Didn't you hear? You won."

"That's impossible," Buddy said. "How could I have won if I didn't even enter! I'd never do anything like that."

Kim felt strangely deflated. "You wouldn't?" she asked.

"I thought the contest was a stupid idea. They were merchandising you like a piece of meat."

Kim suddenly realized that if Buddy hadn't entered, then in all probability he wasn't her mystery caller. "Buddy, this may sound like a stupid question, but have you ever called my show to request songs?"

"No."

"Are you sure?" Kim was beginning to feel a little disappointed.

"Of course I'm sure. And, Kim," Buddy continued, "about my feelings about that contest—I didn't want to say anything bad about it. That would have only made things worse, I think— after the council vote and all."

"I didn't much like the idea either," Kim said quietly.

"Then why did you do it?"

"To help out the station. One night isn't much to sacrifice for a worthy cause."

"So you think a night out with me would be a sacrifice on your part?" Buddy asked. "Thanks a lot."

"You said you didn't enter the contest."

"But someone entered my name. I wonder who?" he asked. "I can't imagine any of my friends pulling a stunt like that."

"You mean they wouldn't get a laugh seeing you out with me?"

"I didn't say that. I just can't imagine the thought ever entering their minds."

"Your friends don't sound very imaginative," Kim said. "But someone must have put in your name as a joke. Anyway, you don't have to go through with the date, if you don't want to."

Buddy hesitated, and Kim wondered if he was weighing the possibility. "You already announced my name?"

"Everyone else in Laurence heard it—except you," Kim said with a touch of sarcasm.

"I'm sorry I couldn't listen to your show, but I was tied up with student council stuff. I think we'd better go through with it, Kim."

"The date? I really don't want to make you uncomfortable."

"But you've already made the announcement. Think how bad it would look if I didn't show up with you."

"Bad for whom? *You?*" she asked caustically.

"Actually, I was thinking more of you. I'll bet there were a lot of guys really hoping to win that contest. I'm sure they'd be pretty angry if they found out the contest was rigged."

"Hey, we don't know that it was. But I see your point about the date. You were named the winner, so you'll have to go out with me. It's as simple as that."

"Right," Buddy agreed. "A simple arrangement. I'm willing to do my part—you're willing to do yours. So it's all set. I'll pick you up tomorrow night at eight, OK?"

"I'll be waiting," Kim told him. But inside she wondered what she was really getting herself into—and where it was all going to lead.

The following morning Kim was in the middle of eating her breakfast when she got a phone call from Vic. "I wanted to see if you'd recovered from yesterday. You were pretty shocked when you left the station."

"Well, Buddy Forward was the last person in the world I expected to win."

"The last person anyone thought," Vic echoed. "My sympathy's with you. I know how rough it's going to be for you tonight."

"Oh, I'll be able to survive," she said. She was actually looking forward to the date now, wondering whether she and Buddy would be able to stand being with each other for an entire evening.

"A date with Buddy's bound to be torture for you—"

Kim cut Vic off. "You say that as if you *want* it to be awful for me."

"Of course I don't," Vic insisted. "I just know how you feel."

"Do you?" Kim asked, a bit resentful. "What if I told you I wanted to go out with Buddy?"

"I'd say you were lying. Come on, Kim, you can be honest with me. You're really dreading it, aren't you?"

"No," she said, eager to hear Vic's response.

"You're not?" he asked, surprised.

"Not at all," Kim said, enjoying his reaction.

"Buddy's not so bad. He's kind of cute, and he's friendly to talk to. I bet he can even dance, too."

Vic still didn't believe her. "Oh, Kim, you'll do anything for the station, won't you? I just want to let you know that I'll be around if you need me."

Kim was growing angry. "What makes you so sure I'll need help? I'm perfectly capable of handling myself."

"Oh, I know that," Vic said, sounding a little desperate. "But I also know that Buddy isn't your idea of a good time. If you find yourself going a little crazy being around him, I'll be waiting for you."

"Don't bother," Kim told him. "I intend to see this one through, for better or worse."

"You're very brave, Kim."

Suddenly something occurred to Kim. "Vic, you wouldn't have had anything to do with entering Buddy's name in the contest, would you?"

"Gee, why would you say that?"

"Well, it seems too pat. Your calling me up practically pleading for me to spend part of tonight with you. You want me to have a lousy time at the dance, and no one better to do that with than Buddy, right?"

"You're hardly friends, you know," Vic said.

"You rigged the contest, didn't you!"

"Well—sort of," he admitted. "But not how you think."

Kim was appalled. "How could you?"

"I did it for you, Kim. I wanted to get another chance with you."

"But how many times have I told you we're through?" she cried.

"You seemed awfully interested to meet a certain guy who kept calling your radio show."

"*You* were my mystery boy?" A wave of disappointment swept over Kim. "I never would have guessed."

"I know. But once I got started, I couldn't figure out how to reveal myself to you. Then when the station controversy blew up, I got this idea about the contest. I thought it'd be perfect. I'd be in control of all the entry forms, and I'd fix it so you'd pick me as the winner. But last week Mr. Block caught me stuffing the box and really gave it to me. He said that if I won the contest, he would expose the fraud and cancel the dance. But I didn't like the idea of anyone getting the chance to date you—especially if it turned out to be someone you really liked. So I stuffed the box with Buddy's name instead. I figured he'd be a safe choice."

"Well, thanks for your concern, Vic," Kim said icily. "It's so nice to know I have such good friends watching out for my welfare. At least Buddy has honesty and integrity and brains—all of which you obviously lack. Goodbye, Vic." Amazed at Vic's audacity, she slammed the phone down.

Her thoughts then turned to the boy she'd be spending the evening with—Buddy. She'd really built him up just then. Now she wondered how much of it she really meant.

Chapter Eleven

Jennifer marched out of her bathroom and posed for Kim. "So what do you think?" she asked.

Kim smiled. The rust-colored jump suit complimented Jennifer's reddish-brown hair, and its stylish lines suited her perfectly. "I think Alan's going to love it," Kim said, referring to Jennifer's new boyfriend. "You look great."

"Thanks." Jennifer slumped her slender body against her dresser. "I appreciate it. It took me days to find this."

"Well, you look fantastic." Kim sighed. "Now if only I can figure out what to wear tonight."

Jennifer couldn't believe her ears. "It's two o'clock, Kim," she said. "How can you wait until the last minute to think about something so important?"

Kim leaned back against Jennifer's wicker headboard. "Well, I was all set to wear this little scarf dress I picked up at the Red Parrot. But I don't feel right about wearing it now. I don't think Buddy will like it."

Jennifer raised an eyebrow. "What does he have to do with it? He didn't even want to win this date. Why go out of your way to please him?"

Kim shrugged. "I don't know, Jennifer. I've been asking myself the same thing all day. There's no reason in the world I should do anything to make him feel comfortable, yet when I took the dress out of my closet this morning, I didn't feel right about wearing it. Like it was a little too wild. It's crazy, isn't it?"

Kim was sure that Jennifer was about to say "Yes it is." But then her friend grew thoughtful. "Maybe it's not so crazy, Kim. How do you really feel about having to spend tonight with Buddy?"

"Oh, you know," Kim shot back. "Buddy's the last person I'd want to hang out with." But even as she said the words, Kim was questioning how much she really meant them.

Jennifer sensed Kim's doubt. "I don't believe you. That may have been true a month ago, but I'm not so sure anymore. I think you're glad things worked out this way. Admit it, Kim."

Admit it? Kim thought wildly. How could she admit it to Jennifer when she couldn't admit it to herself? Yet it was true that she hadn't been able to stop thinking about Buddy since she announced his name on the air. She had meant everything she'd said to Vic about Buddy. Without realizing it, she'd begun to see him in a new light. She wanted this date to work and didn't want to do anything that would jeopardize their having a good time with each other.

"Well, am I right, Kim?"

Kim looked up at Jennifer, who had changed out of the jumpsuit and had put on a pair of jeans. She was pulling a Laurence High T-shirt over her head. She didn't know how long she had been sitting there thinking about Buddy, but by the impatient look on Jennifer's face, Kim imagined it must have been awhile. "I guess you're right," Kim admitted. "I don't know how I ever managed to get myself into a situation like this. And no matter what you say, it *is* crazy."

"Why?" Jennifer asked. "You're a girl, and he's a boy. Things like this have been going on since the beginning of time."

"Not between opposites like us."

Jennifer snickered. "Just because he's smart and handsome doesn't mean you have to treat him like a leper. It's honorable to have compassion for those below you."

Kim took one of Jennifer's pillows and squeezed it between her knees. "But what if I don't think I'm better than he is? All this time it's been so easy to put him down. He was in his own little world, doing the things he liked to do. I was in mine, doing what I liked. It was even fun to say nasty things about him and get a laugh. But I've been doing an awful lot of thinking,

Jennifer, and I see now how much of that teasing was because of jealousy. Buddy is a pretty remarkable guy."

"And you don't think you have anything to offer him," Jennifer finished for her. "Or that your frivolous party dress won't have enough class for him. I know what you're thinking, Kim, and you should get those thoughts out of your mind right now. You may not realize it, but you're a pretty remarkable girl yourself. Doing three radio shows a week, busting your chops to get support for the station, and still having time for your friends and school. Buddy should be proud to take you to the dance."

Kim looked down at the pillow. "You're a real good friend, Jennifer," she said. "I know I ought to stop feeling nervous about myself, but I genuinely want things to go right tonight."

"Then do what you've been doing all along— just be yourself. If there's anything I know about Buddy, it's that he hates a phony. If you pretend to be anything other than yourself, you might as well kiss him goodbye right now."

"You're right, Jennifer."

"You bet I am. You're pretty lucky that things worked out this way. There are plenty of girls in school who'd kill to be in your shoes."

"My shoes? Jennifer, you just reminded me. I never checked to see if I had any shoes that go with that dress!"

"The scarf dress?" Jennifer asked.

Kim nodded. "Want to come over to my house and help search my closet?"

Jennifer threw her arm across Kim's shoulder. "With pleasure, *amigo*. Come on, we don't have much time. . . ."

Chapter Twelve

"**K**im, I've never seen you so nervous. Are you sure you'll be all right?" Mrs. Belding asked as Kim finished getting ready for her date.

"I'm fine, Mom," Kim said while trying to get the post of a red-laquered earring into her left ear. Her shaking hands missed the hole, and she dropped the earring into the bathroom sink.

"Do you need help with that?" Mrs. Belding asked.

"Mom, I'm *fine*," Kim repeated, picking up the earring with newly polished fingernails. As she guided the post through her ear, she heard the sound of the front doorbell. Kim jumped with excitement.

Her mother patted her reassuringly. "I'll answer it. And, Kim, you look beautiful," she added.

"Thanks, Mom." The compliment calmed Kim down a little. Her mother had been a bit wary when Kim had come home with the dress she was now wearing. But Kim knew that the dress, made up of scarves sewn artfully together, was well suited to her small body. Its jagged hemline showed off her slim and petite legs to their best advantage. But what would Buddy think? She'd find out any second now.

She felt so silly and self-conscious inside. *I've got to relax*, she told herself. Taking a deep breath, she bounded out of the bathroom, scooped up her red shoulder bag from her bed, and walked toward the living room, where Buddy was talking with her parents.

Kim paused outside the doorway. Something about Buddy seemed different. Kim examined him closely. His short blond hair was combed neatly as usual, the pale blue sweater he wore fit him well. His jeans—

That's it, she realized, smiling. Kim couldn't remember ever having seen Buddy wear jeans. They looked brand-new, too. She wondered if he'd bought them just for their date. They weren't exactly what she'd call high fashion, but it was clear to her that Buddy was trying. It made Kim feel great. She thought that Buddy must feel something for her to have gone to all that trouble.

"Hi, Buddy," Kim called cheerfully as she approached him. "I see you've met my parents."

He nodded and smiled, showing off his gleaming teeth. "I brought this for you." He opened a small box to reveal a smooth white orchid.

Kim was genuinely touched. No one had ever given her a corsage before. "Thank you," she said, taking the flower out of the box. "Kind of old-fashioned, but I like it. Part of your politeness package?"

Buddy ignored Kim's last comment. "It's the kind that goes on your wrist," he said. "I thought since you were the guest of honor, you ought to have something special."

"That was very thoughtful of you," Kim said. The nervousness she'd felt while she was getting dressed was coming back. Her words seemed stiff and forced.

"Here, let me help you." Stretching the elastic wristband, Buddy guided the corsage onto Kim's left wrist. Despite herself, Kim felt a rush at the touch of Buddy's fingers on her arm.

"All set," Kim said with a nervous giggle. "Shall we go? May as well get it over with." She glanced up quickly to see if Buddy had responded to that remark. She didn't really mean it, but she was still very anxious about letting her true feelings show.

But Buddy didn't challenge her. It was obvious that he took the remark seriously when he wiped the smile from his face and took a few steps toward the door.

"You're right," he answered tersely. "My car's out front." He held the door open for Kim, and they walked down the flagstone path to the side-walk.

"This is your car?" Kim said, looking at the old Mustang. It was a stupid thing to say, she realized at once, but she felt a little funny now about having hurt his feelings. Maybe she should open herself up a little. "It's nice," she added.

Coming up behind her, Buddy opened the passenger door. "It's old, but it's reliable," he said.

For an old car it was in good condition. The vinyl interior was shiny and spotlessly clean, and the sheepskin seat covers were comfortable and warm. "I've been able to fix it up with the money I've made from the Shop Mart," Buddy continued after he'd started up the engine. "I just had a new sound system put in."

"I'd like to hear it," Kim said.

Buddy turned on the radio and caught the middle of a popular rock song. The system was good—very good—Kim thought, a little surprised that Buddy would care about such things. Looking down at the radio, she noticed that it was tuned to a station at the left of the dial. "You've got on K-LAU!" she exclaimed, surprised. "I see you're still being polite to me."

"I don't understand."

"Well, it was awfully considerate of you to put the station on for me."

"At the risk of offending your ego, I must

admit I was listening to the station on my way over here. That Rex Corona's terrific."

"You mean you've started to listen to K-LAU? I thought you thought we were all a bunch of no-good jerks."

Buddy laughed. "Did I really say that?"

"Something to that effect. Anyway, you told me you never listened."

"I never did—until this whole controversy began. Honestly, I'd based my whole opinion of the station from what Heather told me. But after you got so mad at me that first time we talked, I realized it was wrong of me to be so judgmental without firsthand knowledge. So I started listening. I think I like Rex's show the best, with all those funny records. He reminds me of Dr. Demento."

"Yeah, Sean's a pretty crazy guy," Kim agreed.

"Who's Sean?"

"Sean Englund, alias Rex Corona. Don't ask me why he changed his name. I guess he liked having the other identity. But I don't know for sure. He's one of the guys who just comes in, does his show, and leaves. He even does his own engineering because he doesn't trust anyone else to touch his records. Pretty strange, if you ask me." Kim covered her mouth. "Whoops, what am I saying? I'm giving you ammunition for your argument."

Buddy turned to her and smiled. "Don't worry, Kim. I think I went a little overboard in my criticism. I've checked out your show, too. You're very good." He bit his lip. "Heather would die if she heard me say that."

Kim stared straight ahead at the traffic on State Street. It was easier for her to look at the headlights of the oncoming cars than to look at Buddy. He still scared her, and she wasn't sure she could believe what he was saying. "I guess she doesn't like me too much."

"I'd hardly think that would be news to you."

"You two are pretty close, aren't you?"

"Not really. We're still friends, but I stopped going out with Heather months ago."

"Why did you break up with her?"

Buddy rapped his fingers on the steering wheel. "Would you believe me if I told you she was too predictable?" He grinned. "She sure didn't when I told her. In a way, I think I found it hard to believe myself. I mean, everyone in school was going around saying what a perfect couple we were, how suited we were to each other. It was fine for a while, but then we got stuck in a rut, always doing the same things with the same people. I started to get bored, but Heather didn't see anything wrong. She took it really hard." He paused, putting the car in neutral as they stopped for a red light. "Uh, I guess I'm boring you with all this."

"Not at all," Kim said, facing him. "I always wondered what had happened."

Buddy took her arm. "Now you're being the

polite one, Kim. Let's not talk about Heather anymore."

"OK, what should we talk about then?"

There was an awkward pause as both Kim and Buddy searched their minds for a topic. Kim flashed briefly on the image of the two of them standing around the dance floor all night like a pair of statues. But before she had a chance to dwell on the image, Buddy spoke up. "Let's talk about you," he said. "In a way I'm kind of glad we're doing this. I want to find out what Kim Belding does with her life other than play records—and yell at student council presidents." Buddy grinned.

Kim was glad to see that Buddy was being friendly. But what could she tell him about herself? "I suppose I'm just an ordinary sixteen-year-old—" she began.

Buddy cut in. "You're anything but ordinary, Kim," he said, this time without the joking smile.

"Oh, I don't know about that," Kim went on, becoming more serious. "I do my schoolwork; I spend too much time shopping at the mall and talking on the telephone. When I feel like exercising, I knock a few balls around the tennis courts. Sometimes I baby-sit for the couple next door. Just like any other girl."

"But you're not," Buddy insisted.

As they pulled into the school parking lot, the sounds of the dance music could already be heard. About a dozen other couples from the parking lot were making their way toward the auditorium entrance. "Looks like we're right on time."

Kim opened her door before Buddy could reach it and met him near the hood of the car.

"Like I was saying, you're not ordinary. You're independent and strong, not afraid to try out new things."

"You aren't, either, I see," Kim noted.

"What do you mean?"

"Your being here with me. I know it's a big effort on your part, and I just want you to know how much I appreciate it."

Matching each other step for step, they headed toward the dance. "I guess I can say the same thing about you. I hope you're not embarrassed to be seen with me."

"Why should I be? You won the contest—everybody knows that. They're all expecting me to be with you."

"You didn't answer my question. But that's all right," Buddy said. "Before we go in I think you should know this." He grabbed her fingers and squeezed them gently. "I didn't have to go out with you tonight."

"Sure you did," Kim said. "You were obligated to the other contest winners. You need to see this thing through for better or worse."

"Is that the way you feel, Kim?" Buddy asked.

Kim looked into his eyes. Even in the dark she

could see they were serious and pleading. But now wasn't the time to be serious, she felt. "Let's not talk about this now," she told him. "They're waiting for us inside."

Chapter Thirteen

The blast of the music made further conversation impossible. In a way, Kim was glad. She had the strange feeling that something important could be developing between her and Buddy. It was one thing to have thought about it, but quite another to experience it. She wasn't sure if she was ready. There were still several things that had to be resolved—most important of them, Buddy's true feelings about the future of KLAU. From the way he was treating her, Kim had to believe he'd softened his views, perhaps even changed them altogether. But Kim held back from asking about them. It wasn't the time to delve into such serious matters. It was more important that they got to know each other better.

As Kim had expected, all eyes turned to Buddy and her as soon as they entered the gym. She returned the glances with a smile, moving through the crowd with her arm linked through Buddy's. Kim liked the attention, though she realized it would have been considerably less if her date had been any ordinary guy.

Midway across the floor, Kim glanced up at Buddy. He was used to lots of attention and was smiling graciously, showing no signs of discomfort. He looked so cool, so completely at ease with himself. Was it for real, or was it just an act? Kim would have given a million dollars to read Buddy's mind and to be sure.

She imagined the headline in the following week's *Messenger:* "Miracle at Laurence High Dance—Buddy and Kim Together at Last." *No, scratch that,* she told herself. Even though it was a great story, Heather would never put Kim's name in the paper, least of all linked to that of the great Buddy Forward.

"Well, we're here," Kim called out as the two of them arrived at the platform where Vic and Kevin were playing the records. The plan called for Vic to introduce them and have them lead off the next dance.

"It's about time," Vic grumbled. "I was starting to think that you'd skipped this whole thing." Kim sensed some bitterness in his voice.

"It's show time," Buddy whispered.

"You don't mind having to go through with this, do you?" Kim asked. "I think as soon as we start dancing, everyone else will join in, too. Nobody will be staring at us too long."

"Oh, I don't mind," Buddy said graciously. He led her back to the middle of the dance floor. Seconds later the music stopped, and most of the lights in the room were turned off. A lone spotlight shone on Kim and Buddy as Vic approached the microphone at the center of the platform. His slender fingers curled around the metal base as he spoke. "Good evening, everybody. I'm Vic Pastore, and I'd like to welcome you to the K-LAU fund-raising dance. I'll be your deejay for the evening. On behalf of the station, I want to thank each and every one of you for your support. Thanks to you we've raised a lot of money for K-LAU—enough, we hope, to allow it to remain on the air. We'll find out for sure next week when the school board announces its recommendation. But we've shown them that Laurence really cares about K-LAU, right?"

"Right!" everyone shouted.

"Now, gang, it's now my pleasure to introduce to you our guests of honor for the evening, the winner of the K-LAU contest and his lovely date. Neither one really needs an introduction, but as long as I'm up here let me say—Buddy Forward and Kim Belding. Let's give them a hand."

As applause and cheers rose from the crowd, Vic signaled Kevin to start up the next record. Kim recognized the first few chords of a fast song by Michael Jackson, and she began to dance. She closed her eyes and started to move.

But her eyes flew open suddenly when she felt Buddy pull her arms and twist her around.

"Buddy! What are you doing?" Kim cried out in surprise.

Buddy smiled slyly. "Aren't you up for dancing with me? Or do you plan to solo all night?"

"It's not that," Kim said, pulling back a little. "I just thought—"

"I'll bet you thought I couldn't dance, right?"

"Well, not that you couldn't dance," Kim said, "just that maybe your repertoire was limited."

"There's a lot about me you don't know. I'm not the wimp you make me out to be."

"I don't think—" Kim began.

"You don't have to lie, Kim. I've seen it in your face ever since we met." Then he abruptly changed the subject. "Good turnout," he said, glancing around the room.

"Yes, it's great to see such support for the station," Kim said, relieved that he had changed the subject.

After two more songs ended, Buddy grabbed Kim's hand and started to lead her through the maze of dancers. "Let's go get something to drink. I'm really thirsty."

At the refreshment table next to the disc jockey's stand, Buddy bought two glasses of punch and handed one to Kim. "About what I said earlier," he began. "I've been wanting to tell you that for a long time," he said.

"Why?" she asked, looking away from him. "Why would it matter to you what I think?"

"I've never liked the way you pigeonholed me. The straight-A student, who's too good for anyone, right?"

"Well, aren't you?" Kim asked, fingering her paper cup nervously. Despite her better judgment she and Buddy were having the serious conversation she had wanted to delay.

"I don't know. I've never considered myself a snob—or any of the other things that have been said about me."

"I think it's called guilt by association," Kim said. "You hang around with some people who think they're better than everyone else at school. In case you haven't noticed, Heather and company don't seem to be here. This crowd must not be good enough for them."

"Maybe that proves my point," Buddy said. "I don't consider myself above anyone. But you're right that most of the people who are my close friends didn't plan on coming tonight. It's not their kind of thing."

"But is it yours, Buddy?"

"I'm enjoying myself—a lot."

Kim blushed. "Thanks, Buddy. I owe you an apology." She held out her hand. "Forgive me?"

Buddy smiled warmly. "Sure."

"So far tonight I've learned that the real Buddy Forward is a great dancer and nobody's fool. What else is he?"

"Like the real Kim Belding, I enjoy hitting tennis balls once in a while—though not too well, I'm afraid. I guess I'd like to think of myself as an honest, hardworking, somewhat friendly guy who's smart enough to admit when he's made a mistake."

"And what would that be?"

"Not a what. A who. You weren't the only one with misconceptions. I was really wrong about you, Kim. Before we met I had a picture of you as a crazy, off-the-wall girl who was zoned out from spending her life at a radio station."

"And now?"

"Now I see a pretty, caring, intelligent girl, who's a good dancer and probably spends too much time in a radio studio. And someone I'd like to get to know better."

Buddy clasped her hands and looked into Kim's brown eyes. All Kim had to do was give in, and a second later she'd find herself nestled in Buddy's arms, perhaps even kissing him. But Kim wasn't sure what she wanted, so she stood there, her hands limp in Buddy's, trying to avoid his stare. She knew she should say something, but all her words seemed stuck in her throat. Something was holding her back, the question that was still unanswered. And until she got the answer she wanted to hear, she wouldn't feel comfortable in Buddy's arms.

"Kim, is something wrong? Did I say the wrong thing?"

Kim finally looked up at Buddy. "No, not really, Buddy. Except for one thing. Do you still want to see the school board close us down?"

Buddy dropped her hands. "That's a funny thing to ask me now."

"I don't think so. The station is the most important thing in my life. You don't really think I'd want to kiss someone who's trying to ruin it for me, do you?"

Buddy smiled. "Does that mean you would want to kiss me—under the right circumstances?"

"Yes."

"But under the wrong circumstances, you'd tell me to get lost?"

"Something like that."

"Then all I have to do is say I'm one hundred percent behind the station. That's simple enough."

Kim brightened. "Would you really say that, Buddy?"

"I could," he said coyly. "But how do you know I'm telling the truth?"

"I know that Buddy Forward would never lie. But if you really are ready to support us, you should be willing to go public. I'd like you to get up on the stage with me and tell everyone you're ready to help. It would really mean so much." It would be the perfect ending to a wonderful evening. The night she discovered Buddy.

But Buddy was in no mood to mix romance

with politics. His expression hardened, and he began to pace around Kim. "I've been really stupid, but I see what's been happening now. You've used me, Kim. I was really beginning to think you were terrific, and now you go and pull this."

Kim was frightened by his sudden change of mood. "Buddy! I don't know what you're talking about!"

"Oh, come on, Kim, give me some credit. I see what you're up to now. You don't care about me at all. You probably never have. The only thing you're capable of caring about is your radio station. I suppose I should have seen it coming. You probably engineered this date yourself as a means of trying to win me over to your cause. And it might have worked, too. But I see through your plan now. I'm not going to be used by anyone, Kim!"

Kim was momentarily paralyzed by Buddy's harsh words. *He's got it all wrong,* she cried to herself. She wasn't using him. "Buddy!" she cried out. "Let me explain, please!"

"If you think I'm going to stand around here and let myself get talked into believing your lies, you can forget it," he snapped at her. "I'm getting out of here. I'm sure one of your friends here can see you home." Without saying another word, he stormed out of the gym.

Feeling helpless, Kim stood alone. There was

no point in running after him. In his frame of mind, he wouldn't listen to her anyway. Maybe it was just as well. She'd certainly made a mess of things.

Chapter Fourteen

A few minutes later Jennifer found Kim staring into a mirror in the girls' bathroom. "What happened, Kim?" she asked with genuine concern. "You've been crying."

"I still am, Jennifer," Kim rasped, dabbing yet another piece of paper towel at her reddened eyes. "This is the most miserable night of my life."

"Here, take one of these." Jennifer opened up her satin purse and took out a wad of tissues. "No sense ruining your eyes with that stuff."

"I couldn't care less about my eyes," Kim said, though she gratefully took Jennifer's tissues. "It's my heart that's having the problem."

"What happened?" Jennifer asked. "Would you like to talk it out?"

Kim shrugged. "What about your date?"

"Oh, Alan can wait," Jennifer said casually,

perching herself on top of one of the sink counters. "This is more important."

"Thanks," Kim said. "All I know is that I've just set a record for the shortest love affair in history." She poured out her version of her date with Buddy and how she ruined her would-be romance.

Jennifer offered her another tissue. "Hey, it's all right, Kim. You got burned, and it's not very pleasant, but you'll get over it. When you come right down to it, nothing really happened anyway."

"I know."

"And it was Buddy, after all. The guy you used to love to make jokes about. Nothing's been lost tonight."

"That's what I've been trying to tell myself, Jennifer. But it's not true. I think I always saw things I liked about Buddy—and that's why I'm so miserable now. I've never been able to admit to myself that I really like him—and now it's too late." She threw up her hands helplessly. "It's crazy, Jennifer. It doesn't make any sense to me that I could care about someone who disagrees with me on something as important as K-LAU."

"Then maybe you don't care as much as you thought. K-LAU is the most important thing in your life, certainly more important than Buddy."

"I wasn't even thinking about the station at the beginning of the night. I was having a terrific time with Buddy and getting to see what a

141

great guy he is. He seemed to be enjoying being with me, too. Then, just when he's ready to kiss me, I bring up the radio station! I wanted to kiss him more than anything, yet the only thing I could think about was the station and what a traitor I'd be. Sometimes I wish I'd never heard of K-LAU!"

"Hey, I know you better than that. Buddy let you down tonight, and it hurts, but you've got to deal with it."

"But I can't help but blame myself for pushing him to do something he wasn't ready to do. I think the dance had an effect on him, Jennifer. He was really having a good time. I think he may have changed his mind, but he wasn't going to admit it once he got it into his head that I was playing a trick on him. Now he never will. He'll never speak to me again, either."

"The station will live without Buddy, and so will you, Kim. Maybe in a few days after he's calmed down, you can go up to him and tell him what you told me. If it'll make any difference."

"Maybe . . ." Kim said, but already she was thinking of another way to make Buddy understand.

On Monday afternoon Kim dedicated her entire program to rock's greatest blues artists. She felt it was appropriate; she'd never felt more depressed in her life. The school board was set to make its recommendation on the fate of KLAU

142

at their meeting that Wednesday night. With the broad-based support the station was getting from the town and the sizable amount of money the committee had been able to raise through the on-the-air drive, the contest, and the dance, Vic had grown increasingly optimistic that the board would keep them in operation.

But Kim couldn't share his feelings. Not that day, at least. While sizable, the funds were far short of what would be needed to run the station, and she was no longer sure that their efforts would be enough to impress the board.

Kim was already resigning herself to accepting life without KLAU. Maybe it wouldn't be too hard for her, she thought. The station would still be alive for the rest of the year. Next year she'd be a senior, and she'd try to see if she could get an internship at one of the rock stations in San Diego. She'd even settle for volunteering at KDEH, the other radio station in town.

Kim had no doubts she'd manage just fine, but she never saw her fight to save KLAU only in personal terms. She was just as concerned about the kids still in Laurence Junior High and in the elementary schools, who'd never get the chance to work on a high-school radio station.

Then there was Buddy. He'd passed her in the hall that morning without saying a word. Kim hoped that someday she'd be able to tell him how she felt about him, how she still felt about him.

As it was, she wondered if she'd ever be happy again.

Maybe this is what growing up is all about, she thought. *The realization that things don't always work out the way you want them to.*

It was midway through an Eric Clapton song that Kim decided to make one more try. She tore out of her chair and ran to the music library, thumbing through the stacks for a song that would communicate what she couldn't. She found it, a ballad by Continental Drift that told of a misunderstanding that caused the loss of a love. It might not make a difference, anyway. But if Buddy had any feelings left for her, there was the chance he might be listening. . . .

"We have a request here on the LAU," Kim began as the Eric Clapton song faded out. "This is a special song dedicated to Buddy Forward, made with all sincerity from a heartbroken friend, who's smart enough to know when she's made a mistake."

Kim gave the signal to Rodney to start the record.

Chapter Fifteen

A bright ray of sunlight awakened Kim on Wednesday morning. Groaning, she rubbed her eyes sleepily, stretched her arms over her head, got out of bed, and stumbled over to her window. The sun was shining, and Kim didn't see a cloud in the sky.

But the good weather did nothing to raise Kim's spirits. She didn't feel it was fair that it was so beautiful outside while she was feeling so miserable. She thought she was feeling low on Monday, but when Tuesday passed without her getting any word from Buddy, she felt even worse. She saw no reason to hope he'd talk to her that day, either.

In the past she'd always had the radio station to console her, but just thinking about the station now brought on another wave of depression. That night was the night of judgment, the night of the school board meeting. Mr. Block had spoken to Ms. O'Malley the day before and had sadly reported to the staff that the principal was still strongly opposed to keeping the station alive. He'd talked to other board members who were equally fervent in their support of the station, but all Kim could see now was the dark side.

After school Kim went to the station to do her program. She saw no reason not to continue her tribute to the blues and led off the show with a B.B. King record she'd grabbed hastily from the music library right before going on the air.

It was a good choice. Kim turned the control knob on her monitor speaker up loud and let the soulful tune penetrate. She began to feel a little better. She'd always have the music, even if she might not always have the station. Wiping everything else out of her mind, she let herself be carried away by the old song lyrics.

"Kim, the record's ending," Rodney called out through the intercom. "Do you want the mike, or are you going to play another record?"

Kim was back in her chair, searching the tabletop for the copy she was to read. She felt awful about being so unprepared. It was so unlike her. Yet she remained calm and found the announcements just as Rodney started playing the Schoolbeat theme. No one listening would ever have imagined the panic Kim had just recovered from as she breezily began chatting away about the latest school activities.

As she was informing her audience about the cheerleaders' bake sale, Rodney sneaked into the studio and quietly retrieved the stack of albums Kim had been looking at. He went back to the control room and had another record cued up just as she was about to make her final announcement.

Kim's voice grew serious as she read the words Vic had prepared earlier that day. "And, please, don't forget, tonight at eight-thirty is the meeting of the Laurence Board of Education here at the Laurence High auditorium. As regular listeners to K-LAU are aware, the board is scheduled to discuss the future of K-LAU, a future that is in serious danger. We need you now more than ever, and need you to show that you care by coming to the meeting."

Then Kim set aside the prewritten copy. "You've all been wonderful in your support of this station up to now. All the people who signed petitions, who donated money—we appreciate it in more ways than I can say. Even if you can't make it to the meeting tonight, it's been gratifying to know how much you believe in us. Still, we wouldn't be asking you to come if it weren't so incredibly important. I'm going to be there, and I hope to see you."

Kim stopped as a hand suddenly yanked the microphone away from her. "I hope to see you there, too," she heard. She nearly screamed when she turned around and saw Buddy speaking into the mike, reading from something he'd written in a notebook. "This is Buddy Forward," he continued. "It's not too late to give your support to K-LAU. The station has been an institution at Laurence High for three decades now, and we'd like to see it live on for at least another three decades. It's too valuable a resource to be allowed to let die. I'm going to tell the board that I want K-LAU to stay on the air. I hope you will, too. Thank you."

Kim quickly signaled to Rodney to start up the next record. Then she turned to Buddy and cried out, "What are you doing here?"

"A fair question," he said. "I know that coming out for the station at this late date may not mean that much, but it was something I felt I had to do."

"But I thought you—"

"Yeah, I know. Old conservative Buddy, convinced this place is a waste. That's not entirely true, Kim. I did feel that way at first. But I don't anymore. There is some important learning going on here—and I think the school board can find the money to keep the station going."

"When did you change your mind?"

"Kim, the record's ending!" Rodney called out before Buddy could answer.

Kim was too caught up in her talk with Buddy to switch back to her show. But she knew she was about to leave it in capable hands. "Rodney, you pick out the next record—and the one after that."

"B-but Kim!" he pleaded, waving his arms.

"Don't Kim, me," she called back quickly, "just do it. That's an order, Rodney!" She flicked off the intercom. Rodney might be a little flustered, but she was confident he'd do just fine. She turned back to Buddy.

"What changed your mind?" she asked again.

"I hate to say it, but you did. Slowly but surely, everything you'd been trying to tell me started to make sense. I don't think ninety percent of the kids here put as much effort into school as you do at this place. I see how much you and all the rest of the staff have learned here—maybe even more than in any of the classrooms."

"In my math teacher's class you're more than right. But why did you turn the student council against us?"

"I never did that. Sure, I voted against the resolution, but so did a lot of others on the council. The truth was, it never had a chance."

"But why? Most of the school seemed to be behind us."

"Most of the school isn't friends with Heather Shearson—but a lot of the council members are. And she can be very persuasive." He snickered. "I never told anyone this, but she was the one who talked me into running for council president in the first place. It took me a long, long time to realize that she wanted it more for herself than for me."

"How so?"

"She's on a power trip and had this grand idea about the two of us being in charge of the school together. I never knew how seriously she took it, though, till this whole K-LAU thing blew up. This station is the only place where she didn't have any influence, and that bothered her so much she was willing to do anything to discredit it."

"Like her drive to replace Vic?" Kim wondered.

Buddy nodded. "And blowing the comments you made about me way out of proportion. The school board study couldn't have come at a better time for her. They raised some legitimate arguments, but she didn't even care what they were. All she cared about was having her own way. Unfortunately, I helped her. But not anymore, not on those terms."

"Why are you telling me this now?"

"I was going to tell you on Saturday night. But when it seemed you were giving me an ultimatum, I was sure you were trying to do what Heather had done to me—use me to satisfy your own motives."

"If that's how you feel, why are you here now?"

"I heard your show the other day and began to have my doubts. That's not what you were doing, was it?"

"No, Buddy, I wasn't trying to use you. But I

can understand why you'd think I was. I wanted to explain to you how I felt, but for a long time I didn't understand myself. I never thought I'd want to have anything to do with you, but the you I'd thought that about didn't turn out to be the you who's standing right here now. I guess what I'm trying to say is that I like you, Buddy. As crazy as it seems, I like you!"

Buddy's face lit up. "Then I must be crazy, too, because I think I like you, too."

"You don't know how much I've been hoping you'd say that," she replied.

"In that case, I think we have some catching up to do."

"We do?"

Buddy approached Kim with his arms open and hugged her close. "As I recall, the last time we were together I was just about to kiss you."

"Don't let me stop you," Kim whispered, raising her face to meet his. All the emotion she'd been storing up expressed itself in that kiss, and after their lips parted, Kim felt as though the weight of the world had been lifted from her shoulders.

"What time do you want me to pick you up?" Buddy asked, still holding her closely.

"I didn't know we had a date," Kim said.

"A real hot one. Front-row seats at the school board meeting. I think we ought to get there early. From what I hear, there should be a packed house tonight. How does seven-thirty sound?"

"Wonderful," Kim said just as Rodney opened up her mike and gave her the signal that she had to sign off. Everything was looking up for her now. She even had good feelings about the board meeting. "This is Kim Belding," she said brightly, "signing off on this terrific sunny Wednesday afternoon. Hope your day is as wonderful as mine. I'll be with you again on Friday afternoon. Until then, keep your ears tuned to the LAU."

We hope you enjoyed reading this book. Some of the titles currently available in the Sweet Dreams series are listed on the next page. They are all available at your local bookshop or newsagent, though should you find any difficulty in obtaining the books you would like, you can order direct from the publisher, at the address below. Also, if you would like to know more about the series, or would simply like to tell us what you think of the series, write to:

Kim Prior,
Sweet Dreams,
Transworld Publishers Limited,
Century House,
61–63 Uxbridge Road,
London W5 5SA.

To order books, please list the title(s) you would like, and send together with your name and address, and a cheque or postal order made payable to TRANSWORLD PUBLISHERS LIMITED. Please allow cost of book(s) plus 20p for the first book and 10p for each additional book for postage and packing.

20323 1	P.S. I LOVE YOU (1)	Barbara Conklin	£1.10
20325 8	THE POPULARITY PLAN (2)	Rosemary Vernon	£1.10
20327 4	LAURIE'S SONG (3)	Suzanne Rand	75p
20328 2	PRINCESS AMY (4)	Melinda Pollowitz	£1.10
20326 6	LITTLE SISTER (5)	Yvonne Greene	£1.10
20324 X	CALIFORNIA GIRL (6)	Janet Quin-Harkin	£1.10
20604 4	GREEN EYES (7)	Suzanne Rand	95p
20601 X	THE THOROUGHBRED (8)	Joanna Campbell	65p
20744 X	COVER GIRL (9)	Yvonne Greene	95p
20745 8	LOVE MATCH (10)	Janet Quin-Harkin	95p
20787 3	THE PROBLEM WITH LOVE (11)	Rosemary Vernon	95p
20788 1	NIGHT OF THE PROM (12)	Debra Spector	95p
17779 6	THE SUMMER JENNY FELL IN LOVE (13)	Barbara Conklin	£1.10
17780 X	DANCE OF LOVE (14)	Jocelyn Saal	£1.10
17781 8	THINKING OF YOU (15)	Jeanette Nobile	£1.10
17782 6	HOW DO YOU SAY GOODBYE? (16)	Margaret Burman	75p
17783 4	ASK ANNIE (17)	Suzanne Rand	75p
17784 2	TEN BOY SUMMER (18)	Janet Quin-Harkin	75p
17791 5	LOVE SONG (19)	Anne Park	75p
17792 3	THE POPULARITY SUMMER (20)	Rosemary Vernon	75p
17793 1	ALL'S FAIR IN LOVE (21)	Jeanne Andrews	£1.10
17794 X	SECRET IDENTITY (22)	Joanna Campbell	75p
17797 4	FALLING IN LOVE AGAIN (23)	Barbara Conklin	95p
17800 8	THE TROUBLE WITH CHARLIE (24)	Jay Ellen	95p
17795 8	HER SECRET SELF (25)	Rhondi Vilott	£1.10
17796 6	IT MUST BE MAGIC (26)	Marian Woodruff	£1.10
17798 2	TOO YOUNG FOR LOVE (27)	Gailanne Maravel	£1.10
17801 6	TRUSTING HEARTS (28)	Jocelyn Saal	95p
17813 X	NEVER LOVE A COWBOY (29)	Jesse Dukore	95p
17814 8	LITTLE WHITE LIES (30)	Lois I. Fisher	95p
17839 3	TOO CLOSE FOR COMFORT (31)	Debra Spector	95p
17840 7	DAYDREAMER (32)	Janet Quin-Harkin	95p
17841 5	DEAR AMANDA (33)	Rosemary Vernon	95p
17842 3	COUNTRY GIRL (34)	Melinda Pollowitz	95p
17843 1	FORBIDDEN LOVE (35)	Marian Woodruff	95p
17844 X	SUMMER DREAMS (36)	Barbara Conklin	95p
17846 6	PORTRAIT OF LOVE (37)	Jeanette Nobile	95p
17847 4	RUNNING MATES (38)	Jocelyn Saal	95p
17848 2	FIRST LOVE (39)	Debra Spector	85p
17849 0	SECRETS (40)	Anna Aaron	85p